Murder In Her Mind

Murder In The Shadows #3

Nell DuVall

Published by
Melange Books, LLC
White Bear Lake, MN 55110
www.melange-books.com

Murder In Her Mind ~ Copyright © 2015 by Nell DuVall

ISBN: 978-1-68046-173-2

Cover Art by Stephanie Flint

To my daughters and son, keep writing

Acknowledgements

Thanks to the Internet Writing Workshop, the Central Ohio Fiction Writers, to Novels in Progress, especially Sally Less, Barbara Westerviller, and Janet Slike, Brian, my son and tour director, and Stephanie Darden for her editing. Thanks also to the people of the beautiful Dingle Peninsula. May Ireland always remain timeless, beautiful, and welcoming to all who visit.

Author's Note

Ireland has changed much since my first visit there in the 1980s, and continues to change with its membership in the European Union. Little tearooms have become less common, especially with the requirements for the handicapped and various other EU requirements. Some things have changed little.

After an initial surge in investments and substantial growth, Ireland has shared in the economic malaise of the last ten years. Unemployment is again high. However, the timeless beauty of western Ireland is still there. The legends and history are alive and well, so it's easy to believe in second sight, omens, and the little people. The west of the country offers wonderful music and the local pubs provide real Irish hospitality.

A few Gaelic words appear, the meanings of which are clear from the text. *Bean sidhe* in English is the dreaded banshee, herald of death.

As always, some liberties have been taken. Some places are real, while others are fictional.

The Beginning

Dark clouds gathered in the west. Rising winds whipped angry waves to dash against narrow, rocky fingers stretching into the sea. A violent storm would soon reach land. On the edge of the steep cliff, a dark shape huddled.

The shape resolved into a woman wrapped in a black shawl as she scrambled up the rocks to the narrow path threading its way along the cliff top. She stood on the familiar path a moment and stared at the black clouds massed above the roiling sea.

Ships caught by the storm would have a difficult and dangerous night. She cast a blessing outward. Then, something far out to sea drew her attention. She gasped and clutched the heavy crow pendant she wore.

Writhing clouds shifted and twisted until they revealed the form of a tall woman, dark and menacing. No face or distinct feature was visible. Menace radiated from this shade.

The woman on shore closed her eyes and prayed. The storm would bring disaster and death to those in its path, but her senses warned her the shade threatened change to all she held dear.

"Holy Mother, have mercy," she prayed. "Morrigan, arm those you love and send troubles elsewhere. Keep the Washer Woman far from this servant."

The first drops of rain hit and soon became a torrent that soaked the black wool shawl. Head lowered, the woman hurried away from the violence of the wind-driven rain.

Chapter One

Tula Mohr shuddered and stroked the large sun disk she always wore. A strange unease filled her. She waved a hand as if to banish the spooky feeling.

"Are you okay?" Cassie McLeod, one of her two best friends, stared at her with eyes filled with concern. "This isn't like you."

"It was almost as if an evil wind blew my way," Tula replied. "I haven't any enemies, so far as I know."

"Are you sure?" Leah skewered her with a knowing glance.

"Well, not since you got wounded in the museum." Tula grinned at Leah, remembering that fiasco all too well. "I'm still persona non grata there."

"Yeah, we all know why," Cassie added, grinning.

Leah gave Tula a thoughtful glance. "Not to pry, Tula, but it's been six months since you and Mario Arvila broke up. It's time to move on with your life."

The three women sat at their usual table near the kitchen in Tula's Tea Room, her café on High Street. Cups of Tula's Special Blend scented the air with a mixture of cloves, rosemary, and thyme. Tula sighed and fiddled with the teapot lid as she watched her waitress, Kinesha, serving the several small groups of customers at the square tables near the entrance.

What a treasure that girl was. She could manage without direction. It saddened Tula to realize even her business didn't need her.

She set her mug down with a sigh. "Yes, I should. Trouble is, I don't quite know what I want to do." She stared around the room and counted the customers. Business was about average for this time of day.

"Maybe you should take a trip," Cassie ventured. "Go somewhere different. Isn't there any place you've wanted to go, but never had the time?"

"You forget, I run this place. Who will do the cooking if I'm not here?"

Leah snorted. "Let Kinesha do it, and get another waitress. She's filled in those few days when you've been sick. Why not let her do it for a longer period?"

For a moment, Tula said nothing. "Good waitresses are hard to find."

"That's an excuse and you know it," Leah shot back. "Time to start living and have an adventure. The world's waiting."

Trust Leah to see through pretense. Where would she go? The Tea Room had kept her busy for years. First, it was getting it established, building a clientele, and then finding Kinesha. She hadn't taken a vacation in years. She stroked the spiky golden rays of her sun pendant and let her thoughts wander.

"Ireland," Cassie announced, her blue eyes sparkling and a broad grin on her face.

"Ireland?" Frowning, Tula stared at her for a moment and considered the idea.

In the past, Cassie would have been too shy to suggest something like an overseas trip. She had become more adventuresome since she'd saved Ian McLeod's life, her then future husband, from a vicious killer.

"Didn't you say your father came from there?" Cassie continued. "Some village on the west coast if I remember right."

Tula nodded. "Kilconon. He spoke of it often."

Sipping her tea, Leah challenged Tula with a quirked eyebrow "Okay, that's it. You've never been there, so now would be the perfect time."

Surprised, Tula frowned as she considered such a trip. "I've no idea why we never went to Ireland."

"Don't you want to see it? Maybe you have some long-lost relations there."

"My father never mentioned any relatives, or even friends, Leah. He painted colorful word pictures of Ireland, but he never once mentioned any one beyond his mother. I don't remember him ever visiting there, but then I was away at school in Switzerland for several years."

He'd been an only child like her. Yet even so, he must have had an aunt, uncle, or maybe cousins, yet he never mentioned any. Her mother, a tall, beautiful Somali, never spoke of Ireland, Irish relatives, or any family either. Tula remembered her mother sometimes mentioning her Somali grandmother, but no one else. She shifted uneasily in her chair and lifted the teapot lid to check how much tea remained.

"You look sort of lost," Leah said. "Just think about it. I want the old Tula back. Since Mario married my sister-in-law, you've acted as if the world ended. Getting away will clear your mind and might even turn up a new relative or two."

Tula dismissed that with a wave of her hand. "You're being melodramatic. It's not as if Mario and I were engaged or anything. We liked each other, that's all. Besides, I'm much too busy to go anywhere."

"The breakup hit you hard all the same." Cassie reached for Tula's left hand. "You've always been the one to call it quits in the past."

"Umm, well maybe once or twice." Tula half-grinned at her.

"Uh-uh, more like a dozen or so." Leah winked at Cassie and they both laughed.

Joining the laughter, Tula soon had to wipe tears from her eyes. "You two flatter me."

"No, I never do that," Cassie insisted. "Seriously, call a travel agent and go. Kinesha can manage. If you're really worried, I can stop in and check how things are going for you."

"Look, I'll read the cards for you," Leah offered. "If nothing else, you need a change of scenery. Meet new people, do new things. Hey, maybe you can even collect some Irish recipes for the menu."

"Yes, the cards helped me," Cassie added with a grateful smile at Leah. "Where's your sense of adventure?"

"Alive and well." Tula paused a moment. "Well, let's see what Leah's cards say first, and I'll think about it."

"Deal." Leah shook Tula's hand as Cassie grinned at both of them.

* * * *

Once settled in her seat on the plane, Tula stared out the window, but didn't focus on the bustle outside that accompanied departure.

Ireland was a long way, with seven or more hours in the air. First, she had to transfer to an Aer Lingus flight in Boston. She sighed and her thoughts turned toward her father.

Images filled her mind—her father talking of Kilconon with fondness in his voice, her mother singing a lullaby of love, her parents embracing and kissing as they tucked her into bed. Despite the years since their deaths, she still missed them both. She wanted a relationship with the same warmth and caring her parents had—either that or none at all. She thought, for a while, Mario would provide it, but then his interest waned and they separated. Now she needed a new direction. Maybe Ireland would provide it.

Sometimes she was convinced she had never been an innocent, even as a young woman. The Swiss academy she attended provided a thorough education as well as insisting on proper etiquette, manners, and short excursions to broaden each student's horizons. Tula could never remember being as naïve as her friend Cassie once was. In many ways, she felt more in tune with Leah's almost European healthy cynicism. Her parents' attitudes probably contributed to that as well. With their deaths, she had no choice but to take charge of her life.

Until she passed the age of thirty, she had flirted outrageously and left many a swain battered and bruised in spirit. Mario had been the first man to make her think about marriage. However, that was not to be. She was now even more uncertain about marriage. Being single and independent had its benefits.

* * * *

Tula stared out the plane window at the clouds shrouding the Irish coast and waited for her first glimpse of her father's birthplace. Leah's reading of the Tarot cards swamped her memory.

"You will find that which is lost, and love will claim your heart," Leah had said with an ironic grin on her face.

"Humph. Leah, this is me, remember? I'm not looking for love. I'm looking for a village and maybe a cousin or two, at best. Tell it to me straight."

Grin fading, Leah nodded. "Hey, I just read 'em like I see

'em. The Lovers closed out the reading."

"Enough," Tula sputtered. "I'm not, I repeat, I'm not looking for a man."

"Yeah, but with you there must be one lurking somewhere." She gave Tula a crooked grin. "Anyway, the cards also hint you might find a cloud or two on your trip. I've heard Ireland gets a lot of rain. My best guess is the loss I saw in the cards means your lost relations. So far, I didn't see any disaster looming, so enjoy your trip."

At the airport, Leah and Cassie had hugged Tula and pushed her toward the queue waiting to clear the baggage checkers.

"Bring us back one of those Irish ring shawls," Leah said. "I've always wanted one."

"Enjoy," Cassie added with a hug.

After one last good-bye from Leah, Tula moved forward and presented her ticket and passport to the checker guarding the entrance to the gate area. The woman had looked at the ticket, flipped to the photo in the passport, and then compared Tula to it.

"Better take your shoes off, honey."

Now, Tula gazed out the aircraft window waiting for some sign of land to emerge.

Clouds obscured the view, and land only appeared just before touchdown. All she could see were other planes and a few strips of grass. Just another airport. She sighed and hoped she'd see more after she found a bus to Dingle. The town was quite a distance from the airport according to the guidebook. All she had to do was find where the bus pick-up was located. The Dingle Tourist Information Center could point her toward a B&B or a hotel.

Tula retrieved her carry-on bag and raincoat from the overhead bin and then followed the other passengers to passport control. Traveling light had benefits and she expected to buy some things as she traveled. The officer asked the usual questions, stamped her passport, and waved her through. She took the *Nothing to Declare* exit.

Outside in the lobby area, a horde of people waved signs and looked for new arrivals. Tula paid little attention to them except for one tall, dark-headed man holding a sign labeled *Kelly*. Handsome and tall, with a pair of bright sea blue eyes, he made her wish her name was Kelly.

"Hey, Gen," a man's voice yelled from behind. "That must be us."

The dark-haired man with the sign moved closer to the exit and held his sign higher. The couple behind Tula pushed forward and a bump from something knocked her sideways and into the arms of the waiting stranger.

The stranger acted at once and caught Tula, righting her and preventing a nasty fall. Stunned, she lost herself for a moment in the man's intense gaze.

"Are you all right, ma'am?" He had a warm Irish voice, a bit like her father's.

"What?" Tula regained her footing and righted herself.

She stood eye to eye with the man. Usually she towered over most people. A firm grip reminded her of his help.

"Yes, I'm fine. No damage done."

She took a step away, and the stranger's grip released her. A warm tingle remained where his fingers had rested. Tula sighed.

Then the reality of the airport brought her back to less pleasant things. The long flight had sapped her energy, and she touched her sun pendant for reassurance. A good meal, a hot shower, and a night's sleep would help a lot. Instead, she faced a long bus ride.

"Oh, ma'am, so sorry," a male voice said. "I didn't mean to…"

The Kellys stood to either side of her. The man, of middle height with a slight paunch, gazed at her with worry. He pushed a heavily loaded baggage trolley. The woman, Gen, short and round with hazel eyes, brushed at Tula with a lace handkerchief.

"I hope Jerome didn't hurt you. He's such a klutz. He's so anxious to be on the 'Old Sod,' he's clean forgot his manners. I'm Geneva Kelly. We're from Pittsburgh." She held out a hand.

Tula shook it, noting the woman's firm grip. "Tula Mohr, Columbus." She smoothed her green tunic straight and smiled back.

"What a lovely name," Geneva said. "We've come for a grand tour, but first we're going bird and whale watching with Captain Kehoe."

7

"Welcome to Ireland, Mr. and Mrs. Kelly and… Miss Mohr. Right you are." Captain Kehoe's Irish brogue and melodic voice soothed the ear. "I'm Cap'n Kehoe, at your service. I have a van to take you to Dingle, if you're ready."

"Dingle?" Tula stared at him. "That's where I'm going. Can you tell me where I find the bus?"

"Bus? Fiddlesticks," Geneva said. "Come with us. You have room don't you, Captain?"

"Sure, we can fit her in. Be glad to take you there. If you'll all just wait at the island outside, across from the exit, I'll pull the van up and load the luggage."

"How much?" Tula said. No matter the fee, she'd pay. No way would she pass up this offer.

"Nothing," roared Jerome Kelly and placed Tula's carry-on on the trolley. "It's the least I can do. If Captain Kehoe requires a fare, I'll pay it. Now, let's be on our way."

Tula put on her raincoat and trailed after as Captain Kehoe led them to the traffic island where he unloaded the luggage from the trolley. "I'll be back in a trice. Just bide here."

The cool gray air made Tula glad she'd packed several sweaters and that the raincoat had a hood. She tightened the belt on the tan raincoat, glad for its warmth. The weather in Boston had been hot and steamy. Shannon's gray skies came as a cool and welcome surprise, although she hoped no rain would follow.

* * * *

The trip through the Irish countryside passed in a green blur. Tula tried to keep her eyes open, but the effects of jet lag and a sleepless flight defeated her. Even Mr. and Mrs. Kelly stopped their incessant chatting and slept for a time. She soon nodded off.

The sudden cessation of motion woke her. After two hours of driving, the van had stopped before a quaint little cottage. A sign by the road read *Cream Teas.*

"I thought a cup of tea would not go amiss. Long flights always leave me thirsting," Captain Kehoe said as he held the door open.

"Suits me." Geneva Kelly scrambled toward the door. Her husband woke with a start and stared around as if wondering where he was.

After assisting, Mrs. Kelly, Captain Kehoe held out a hand to Tula and steadied her as she ducked past the van door to step down to the ground. That same electric tingle shot from her hand and along her arm. The captain's blue eyes and broad grin offered a challenge Tula did her best to ignore.

They faced a low stone cottage with a thatched roof. Colorful flowerbeds with yellow roses and bright orange day lilies framed the small porch. It reminded Tula of the guidebook pictures. At the entrance to the stone cottage, a woman wearing a yellow apron smiled at them.

"You'll be wanting the usual tea, Captain?"

"Indeed, Mrs. Doyle, but it's tea for four today."

"Sit anywhere," she said and hurried off.

Inside, Captain Kehoe led them to a table by the window and held a ladder-backed chair, first for Mrs. Kelly, and then one for Tula. The chairs with their rush seats reminded her of her own Tea Room. Once seated, she gazed about the pleasant room. Chintz curtains framed the windows and matching tablecloths and napkins covered the six tables. Peat stacked in the fireplace looked ready for a match. The rain had ceased and bright sunlight shone through the side windows. A china cup and saucer and a small plate in a chintz pattern sat at each of the four places at their table. Altogether, it made a cheery welcome to Ireland.

Soon, Mrs. Doyle returned with a tray of small sandwiches, scones, jam, and cream. A young girl followed with a large, yellow pot of tea, a pitcher of milk, and a bowl of sugar.

"Thank you, Mrs. Doyle." Captain Kehoe gave her a broad smile. "Now, for your first lesson in Irish culture. We like our tea strong, too strong for some Americans. If you prefer it less strong, either ask for weak tea or dilute it with a little hot water. Second, you always add milk to your cup first, and then tea. Most Irish also like a bit of sugar. Never use or ask for cream for tea. Our milk is plenty rich enough."

"Why milk first?" Tula stared at him, puzzled.

"Can't say exactly, but it tastes different if you do it the other way. Anyway, that's how most Irish do it. Who takes milk?" Mrs. Kelly raised her hand.

"All right." He poured the milk, then the tea, and passed her the cup.

He poured one for Tula and then one for Mr. Kelly.

Tula sipped hers and grimaced. "Yes, it's strong all right." She poured more milk into the cup and added a packet of sugar crystals. After a quick stir, she drank a little.

"Ah, that is good."

"Next time put the milk in first." Captain Kehoe grinned at her. "Now, the cream teas are English, but we make them better. There's nothing like a flakey Irish scone, and Mrs. Doyle makes the best. Too, she makes her own raspberry jam, although her blackcurrant is even better."

He picked up a scone, split it, spread both halves with yellow butter, jam, and piled on a dollop of cream last. He passed it to Mrs. Kelly.

She bit into it and smacked her lips. "I love cream teas." The others followed suit.

"I'm surprised to see whipped cream instead of clotted cream," Tula said.

"It's the American influence, you see, and the Irish aim to please." Captain Kehoe lathered his own scone. "The tourist trade, especially the Irish Americans, keeps our economy healthy. However, clotted cream is more English than Irish."

"Any other tips on Irish eating habits?" Tula said, surprised he focused on the food and how to eat it. Then, she remembered all those food-oriented travelogues.

"Yes, we like our sandwiches made fresh," Captain Kehoe continued. "Americans usually ask for salad dressing or mayo, but most Irish prefer just rich Irish butter. However, you'll not find Irish soda bread as common as it once was, but our dark bread is excellent and healthy too. Coffee is served mainly at night, although some have taken to drinking it in the morning too. You can find espresso in most cities. Of course, Ireland produces the finest potatoes, salmon, and lamb in the world. Our beef is also prized."

She raised an eyebrow at that assertion. "Anything you don't do well?"

"Watch the peas, sometimes they come out as mush. The English love their mushy peas."

Tula poured a second cup of tea, careful to pour the milk first.

Captain Kehoe grinned his approval and she smiled back.

"We still have a way to go, so the ladies may wish to visit the loo first. I'll call ahead to let the B&B lady know when we'll arrive. Can I reserve a room for you, Miss Mohr?"

Considering the offer, Tula nodded. "Yes, please do. I won't have to hunt for one when we arrive."

Tula finished her tea, and she and Mrs. Kelly adjourned to the loo. It pleased Tula to see how clean Mrs. Doyle kept the place.

Captain Kehoe fascinated her. Those twinkling eyes of his showed a sense of humor. Maybe she should sign up for a bird watching trip on his boat.

Chapter Two

Finished with tea, they returned to the van. Despite Tula's intention to stay awake, she nodded off again. She woke as they descended a hill and approached the sea. White caps washed the shore where the emerald green of the pastures ended and a gray shingle began. It had been a long time since Tula had seen the sea. The timeless beauty of the landscape refreshed her soul.

A series of loud honks sounded behind the van. Tula peered out the back window to see a red sports car hovering close to the van's bumper. The driver kept sounding the horn.

Captain Kehoe cursed under his breath, but pulled as close to the side of the narrow road as he could. The red vehicle roared past on the wrong side of the road. Tula breathed a sigh of relief and hoped never to see that car or its driver again. She wanted to enjoy Ireland, not become an accident statistic.

"Do all the Irish drive like that?" Geneva spoke in a tremulous voice. "Driving on the left is bad enough without dealing with reckless drivers."

"Too right," Captain Kehoe replied, clearly not happy. "Young hot heads have no place on the roads. I suspect the Garda will take care of him. Many of our roads, especially around the Dingle Peninsula, are narrow lanes with only occasional pull-offs. We also have a lot of slow lorries and farmers' tractors. Don't worry, I know the roads well."

Ahead the road wound around toward a cluster of colorful buildings strung out along the bay. "Captain Kehoe, is that Dingle?" Tula called.

"Aye, ma'am, it is. We'll soon reach your B&B. I'm sure you'll like the place. Mrs. Kennedy is known for her generous breakfast table."

"Right now a shower and a bed sound like heaven." Conscious of tight muscles and an ache or two, Tula shifted as much as she could and yawned.

"Wake up, Jerome." Geneva Kelly poked her husband. "We're almost there."

He groaned and leaned forward. "Dingle?"

"Indeed, sir," Captain Kehoe answered.

He turned off the road and drove along the main street lined with shops, restaurants, and pubs. "You'll have no trouble finding a place for dinner. I'll leave you in Mrs. Kennedy's capable hands and collect you in the morning about eight. Will that suit?"

"Yes," Jerome replied and gazed out the window. He waved to people on the street.

Soon the van turned off the main street and went uphill for a mile or so. A Sixties style brick bungalow sat on the right, and the van pulled into the driveway. Somehow, Tula had expected another stone cottage or something more Irish looking. So much for touristy expectations.

Captain Kehoe stopped and shut off the engine. He opened the door and helped Tula out. Time paused for her at the touch of his hand on hers. It lasted only a moment, yet warmth flowed from his fingers to her. She gave him her best smile and his bright blue eyes responded.

Geneva moved forward and drew Captain Kehoe's attention to her. After she climbed from the van, Jerome scrambled out behind her and stretched, first one way and then the other.

"I got a little cramped, first from the plane seats, and then the long ride here. I'm glad we've arrived. Can't wait to get settled, find a real Irish pub, and some Irish stew. The travel agent insisted the Cliffs of Moher are not to be missed."

"Indeed. They're a popular site with tourists and the locals. It's a bit of a ride, but we can stop several places along the way."

Tula turned to look at the B&B. It presented a welcome sight and promised comfort. The house had a vivid green on the door, trim, and wooden shutters at the windows. Lace curtains framed the view. Fuchsia and roses in abundance filled the front garden with color and scent. It offered a pleasant sight for weary travelers. B&Bs offered adequate services with a homey environment, and cost much less than the more elaborate, full-service hotels.

Captain Kehoe knocked at the door. A plump woman with red hair and a freckled complexion answered.

She greeted the captain with a broad smile. "Welcome, welcome."

"Mrs. Kennedy, I have your guests, Mr. and Mrs. Kelly, and Miss Tula Mohr. They'd like to see their rooms and rest a bit. I'll get the luggage."

Mrs. Kennedy held the door open. "Good it is to meet you all. Kelly, that's a fine Irish name, and Mohr sounds like our famous cliffs." The Kellys and Tula nodded.

"It's great to be on the 'old sod,'" Jerome added.

"Is this your first trip to Ireland?" Mrs. Kennedy stopped in front of a wooden board with keys and removed two sets.

"Yeah, and it's been a long time coming," Jerome responded. "Had to wait until my retirement. We're here to see all of it, especially Galway. My granddad came from there."

"That's north of here. Seeing Ireland takes a bit of doing, but I'm sure Connor will take care of that."

"Connor?" Tula looked at their hostess.

"Yes, Connor Kehoe, but you probably call him Captain."

"Yes, we do," Tula said. "It's my first trip too. My father was born in Kilconon and often spoke of it when I was a child. I can't believe it took me so long to make this trip."

"Kilconon, eh? That's a bit of a way from here, but the bus goes there. Now, I'm sure you'd like a wash up and a little rest. Come along and I'll show you to your rooms," Mrs. Kennedy led them toward a long hallway.

"The bath is at the end, and your rooms just along here—"

"No bath in the room?" Jerome looked taken aback.

His reaction brought a smile to Tula's face. She remembered the summer she had backpacked all over Europe and stayed at youth hostels with shared bedrooms and a communal bath. At least here, she wouldn't have to share a bedroom.

"No," Mrs. Kennedy said, as if she had it heard that complaint before. "This is a B&B, not a hotel. We don't serve meals except for breakfast. It's available from seven until ten, and Connor usually comes about eight or so."

After showing them their rooms, Mrs. Kennedy handed them the keys. "I'll just see where Connor is with your bags."

Tula grabbed a lilac towel from the stack on the wooden chest in her room, her toiletries, a washcloth, and the silk jumpsuit from her carry-on. She knocked on the doorframe of the Kelly's room. "I'm for a quick shower unless you want to go first."

"I'll wait on the bags, so go ahead," Geneva said. "I prefer a nice long soak to get all kinks out. These old bones don't like cramped places." She sighed and lay back on the double bed.

Tula nodded, wondering how the Kellys would manage with the double bed. They were generous-sized people.

After the hot shower, she returned to her room and lay on the bed, sympathizing with Geneva and Jerome. The crowded airplane, followed by the van ride, had caused her muscles to cramp too. The hot shower had helped, but stretching full length did the trick. Relaxing, sleep came almost at once.

Hours later, a timid knock at the door woke her. From the angle of the sun, she guessed it was mid-afternoon. She opened one eye and struggled to remember where she was.

"Miss Mohr, are you awake?"

Tula got to her feet and opened the door. Geneva Kelly stood there.

"We're going into town and thought you might like to ride along."

"Sounds like a great idea. Let me comb my hair first."

"We'll meet you in the living room. Oh, I think Mrs. Kennedy called it the lounge."

Ten minutes later, Tula joined the Kellys and a local taxi ferried them into the center of Dingle. Colorful shops, restaurants, and pubs lined the main street. The bright colors charmed and cheered her. Savory smells teased her nose. Fish and chip shops outnumbered the other restaurants. She loved the way the English fried the fish, and expected no less of Ireland. She was looking forward to eating it later.

Some stores bore signs in both Gaelic and English. Tula recalled the Dingle peninsula favored Gaelic, and according to the guidebook, some folks refused to speak English. How they could function in modern society puzzled her. Still, it gave the place its unique character. Other signs also carried French and German.

15

Jerome surveyed the street with avid interest. "You gals explore the shops while I check out the pubs and places to eat."

"Oh, Jerome, can't you think of anything besides eating and drinking?"

"This is Ireland, honeybun. The locals are sure to know the best places to eat. I'll meet you here, say in an hour or so, and we can get some dinner."

"Tula, is that okay with you?"

"Yes. I've nothing planned until tomorrow."

Jerome ducked into the nearest pub as Tula and Geneva strolled along the main street and looked in the colorful shop windows. A lot of tourist knickknacks and postcards filled the nearest windows. None of the goods appealed to Tula. The next shop had a display of fishermen's sweaters from Aran. Cynically, Tula wondered if they came by way of China.

The world was changing so fast. She regretted that native crafts were disappearing everywhere, replaced by machine-made knock-offs. The world-renowned sweaters once had represented the primary source of income for the islanders. Until sometime in the Seventies, Americans and rich Europeans had valued handcrafted items. Some still did, but the craft had declined, along with the population, in some places. With the growth of the Irish economy, other jobs offered better income prospects and had many benefits, although the present economy threatened a return to leaner times. Tula understood the inevitable changes, but still treasured the much rarer handmade items.

A jewelry store on the other side of street caught her eye. It was possible they might have some Irish silver.

"Geneva, I'm going to check out that jewelry shop. Do you want to come with me?"

"Sure. Maybe I'll see something inexpensive to take home."

As they prepared to cross the street, a red Viper flashed past, just missing them. Tula remembered the tailgating red sports car they encountered earlier and its rude driver. The Viper stopped with a squeal just beyond them. The driver, a dark-haired young man, hopped out and crossed to the store.

"Well, I never," Geneva gasped. "He almost hit us and didn't even apologize."

"I hope we won't see him again," Tula replied. "Maybe I should file a complaint with the Garda."

"That's some car," Geneva marveled. "Is it an MG?"

Tula laughed. "No, it's a Dodge Viper, an overpowered, overpriced American muscle car. That young man must have money. It's probably why he hasn't been arrested. I'll bet he pays off the local police and whatever judge or magistrate they have."

"I'm such a dummy when it comes to cars. I can't keep them straight."

"Well, I'm surprised to see it here. We hear so much from the Europeans about low carbon footprints. Guess he doesn't care."

Once safely in front of the jewelry store, they gazed at the display of silver and gold items in the window. A silver necklace with heavy links caught Tula's eye. She loved silver and owned a number of unique pieces. An Irish one would make a wonderful keepsake of her trip.

"Let's go in here." She held the shop door open for Geneva.

Inside, the young man, an Irish Adonis with broad shoulders and black hair, flirted with the female clerk, a pretty girl with freckles on her pert nose and curly auburn hair. Tula considered scolding the young reprobate, but thought better of it. He appeared the type to just shrug it off and likely do worse next time.

As he talked with the girl and held her hands, something about him struck Tula as familiar. His gestures, or the cadence of his speech, reminded of her father. She narrowed her eyes and studied him more closely. The impression faded. Her father was charming, but she didn't remember him as so arrogant or careless of others.

"Tula, look at these," Geneva pointed to an array of Celtic crosses and knots in pins, broaches, torques, and pendants.

She joined Geneva and surveyed the array. Among them, her eye immediately went to the necklace of heavy silver links. Fascinated, she wanted to hold it, to see how it looked on her. Despite her gold sun pendant, she had an affinity with silver. Associated with the moon goddess and Isis, silver had so many arcane aspects. She tried to ignore the necklace and focus on the other merchandise.

The young man lingered, and the clerk smiled at him, obviously enjoying the attention. Tula sighed, young lovers. Had she ever been so naïve? Used to the amorous attentions of most men she met, she had always watched them with amusement and a healthy distrust. It had served her well until she allowed herself to think of Mario as more than a casual acquaintance. So much for that.

With the clerk occupied, they browsed uninterrupted. Then, she realized Geneva was growing impatient. Perhaps she wanted to buy something. Tula approached the clerk.

The young man leaned over and kissed the girl's cheek. "I'll pick you up at eight."

"See you do," she called as he turned to go. "Danny will be waiting if you're late."

His crooked grin amused and intrigued Tula. No wonder he monopolized the girl's attention. Black hair fell in a jaunty wave over his forehead, and dancing brown eyes sparked above a mobile mouth. A gray tweed jacket emphasized broad shoulders. With almost a bow to Tula and Geneva, he swaggered out the door.

Geneva sighed. "A young Russell Crowe, or one of those handsome boys from Britain."

Tula chuckled at the apt observation. "An Irish rogue all right, young and cocky. It's obvious he considers himself a gift to all women."

She turned to the pretty clerk. "You have some nice silver."

"Indeed we do. We specialize in silver pieces from St. Colm's Workshop. They export all over the world. We leave the mass-produced items to others."

Tula nodded with a knowing smile. "I imagine the prices reflect that."

The girl grinned at her, revealing a lovely set of dimples. "That's so, but since the tourist traffic has fallen off this year, we have a wee bargain or two."

"Such as?"

"We're selling the Celtic knot pins at twenty percent off, and the larger pieces somewhat more. Are you interested in anything specific?"

"I think my friend may be interested in the pins."

"Can I help you, madam?" she said, turning to Geneva.

While Geneva made her selections and paid for her purchases, Tula debated whether to ask about the necklace. Something, she wasn't sure what, drew her to it. The rings reminded her of an eclipse of the full moon she had once seen. Umm, the moon?

"And for you, madam?" The clerk, now finished with Geneva, gave Tula a pleasant smile.

"Umm. I was looking at the silver necklace made of rings."

"A lovely piece and solid silver; no cheap plate for St. Colm. It's heavy and perhaps too large in scale and weight for a wee woman, but would suit you well." The girl removed it from the case and handed it to Tula. "Try it for size."

Tula lifted it, admiring the workmanship and the heft of the piece. Her fingers tingled as she slid it over her head. Gazing at it in the oval mirror on the counter, she thought it glowed with a light of its own against the teal silk. She stroked the silver and a feeling of rightness flowed over her.

"Tula, how beautiful." Geneva oohed and aahed as she walked around her. "I only wish I could wear something like that. It makes you look so elegant, so regal. Sometimes I wish I was tall and willowy instead of short and round. Jerome calls me his Mama Bear."

Removing the necklace, Tula set it on the counter with reluctance. "How much?"

The girl eyed Tula and then Geneva. "Irish pounds, Euros, or American dollars?"

"Dollars. Don't forget to include the VAT." Tula held her breath.

"It's a lovely one, and we haven't seen another quite like it." She studied Tula and pursed her lips. "Well... I could let you have it for $350."

Geneva gasped. "I had no idea silver was so expensive."

"It's nice, but I don't know," Tula said. "Perhaps I'll look around the other shops first."

"Silver prices keep climbing in value, and work like this is dear," the girl responded.

"I'll keep that in mind."

Geneva had selected several pins and a small Celtic cross. They waited while the girl put them in boxes. "Tula, you ought to buy that necklace."

"It's lovely, but I've just started my trip."

"Jerome told me if I see something I liked and really wanted it, I should buy it. You might not find another elsewhere."

"He may be right, but they make such pieces for export, so I can probably find something similar on the Internet."

"Not like this," the girl said. "It's one of a kind. Here you are." She handed a package to Geneva and then picked up the silver necklace. The light reflected from it almost blinded Tula.

Geneva started toward the door, but Tula stopped. "Would you take one eighty for it?"

"Ah, it's a beauty all right, but I can't let it go for so little." She opened the case and lifted the necklace.

"One ninety?"

The clerk sighed. "Ah, no, I couldn't let it go for less than three twenty-five."

"Well, thanks anyway." Tula walked toward the open door Geneva held.

"An even three hundred," the clerk called.

"Make it two hundred and you have a deal."

The clerk looked thoughtful. "Business has been slow and we've had the piece a while. It's too dear for most people. You drive a hard bargain. You must have a bit of Irish in you." The clerk placed the necklace on the counter and reached for a box.

"Yes, my father was Irish. He came from Kilconon."

"So does Ewan." She placed the necklace in the box.

"Ewan?"

"Ewan Clare, the young lad who just left."

"Yes, quite the charmer and sure of himself." Definitely not her type. Tula pulled out her wallet and removed two hundred dollars. She handed the money to the clerk. "Dollars all right?"

"Good as gold. I've put in a note on St. Colm and a copy of the bill in the box." The clerk gave Tula the package with a smile. "Come back again."

"Let's find Jerome and sample some Irish cooking," Geneva said, as they left the shop.

Tula nodded, wondering what she might find tomorrow in Kilconon.

Chapter Three

As Connor placed his supper dishes in the sink, a loud knock on the door shattered the quiet. Few people visited this time of the evening. As he walked toward the door, another knock sounded, this one louder and impatient. He opened it to see Ewan Clare, hand raised to knock again. He detested the man, but tolerated him for the sake of his sister, Moira.

"Took you long enough." Ewan pushed past Connor.

"I wasn't expecting company. What do you want?" Connor stood with arms crossed and eyed Ewan with distrust.

"Aren't you going to offer me a wee one?" Ewan dropped into Connor's favorite armchair next to the electric fire.

"There might be a bit of tea left from supper."

"I meant something stronger, a man's drink." Ewan studied his nails.

"With that car of yours, you don't need spirits. What do you want?"

"Moira said you'd be taking out the boat. She mentioned some tourists who came to watch whales."

"Indeed, it's naught to you."

"I thought you might pick up a wee package or two for me."

Anger, hot and deadly, surged through Connor. He clenched his fists and struggled to slow his breathing. He wanted nothing more than to smash the arrogant young face before him. Taking a deep breath, he strained to open his hands. Violence only begat more violence.

"I've told you before I won't help in these filthy schemes of yours. I want no trouble with the Garda. I've enough with the bloody licensing and all the inspections. You'll get no help from me."

"The lease payment comes due soon. I need these goods." Ewan paused a moment. "I hear business is slow these days, and I know you can use some quid. Doing this wee favor would bring more than you'd make from ten tourist trips."

"I don't want your kind of money. You'd best leave, or perhaps you'd rather I called the Garda. I'm sure they'd have an interest in these goods of yours." Connor held the door open and glared at Ewan.

Shrugging, Ewan straightened his jacket, and ambled toward the door. "You know where to find me."

Connor slammed the door and wished the Hounds of Hell would take Ewan Clare. How could Moira have such a cursed brother? She pulled him out of one scrape after another. With that expensive car of his, sooner or later he'd wreck it and leave her to pay the owners. Ewan had already come close to costing Connor his master's license. Working with him almost guaranteed a gaol sentence.

Returning to the kitchen, Connor washed his dishes and carried a last cuppa to the lounge. He sat in his favorite chair, the overstuffed, chintz covered one he'd inherited from his mam. At least in the lamp light, it looked less faded and dingy. Determined to rid his thoughts of Ewan, he considered the willowy American, Tula Mohr.

He still remembered the warmth of her when he caught her at the airport. A nice armful. Her exotic looks fascinated him. Her skin reminded him of milky tea or wet sand after high tide. Those dark eyes of hers promised a world of passion.

He had avoided women since Janet dumped him. She wanted more than a boat captain with an uncertain future. If he wouldn't stay with a promising bank, she wanted none of him. Maybe he'd have the laugh on her with all the business failures of late. Of course, tourist traffic had also fallen off, but he could carry small loads to the islands cheaper than the ferries. However, a cargo business took time and constant effort. He'd much rather take tourists to see the whales and birds and leave cargo for the winter months when the tourists stayed home.

Pushing those thoughts aside, he thought of the American woman. She had the elegant flair of a high-fashion model, almost too perfect to touch. However, she appeared to have a sense of humor. She hadn't treated the Kellys with disdain. Of course, after a long plane ride, no sleep, and then the van ride, none of them had talked much. So far, he liked what he'd seen.

Maybe he could interest her in joining the Kellys for one of their boat trips. The more he considered the idea, the better he liked it. You could tell a lot about people by how they reacted on such trips. He wanted nothing to do with those who insisted on pampering and hated a little damp weather. After all, Ireland was known for its "soft days." It ensured Ireland's "forty shades of green" and its beautiful gardens.

* * * *

The creak on the stairs alerted Moira to Ewan sneaking up to his room. She'd waited until eleven and then gone to bed. She pulled on her robe and slipped on her scuffs. Sure enough, when she opened the door, she caught sight of him trying to slink into his room.

"Home at last? Lose your way, or did the money run out?"

"Uh, I didn't want to wake you, darlin'."

"Sure you didn't. More like you didna want to hear me scold. How many times have I told you? Some night Sgt. Donovan will stop that fancy car of yours and take you to gaol. Then where will we be? Once he sniffs the spirits on you, you'd lose your license and that car for sure."

"You worry over much. Besides, he'd never catch me on that wee bike of his."

"He might block the road. Someday you'll push your luck too far."

Ewan yawned and stretched. "Me bed calls, Moira. See you in the mornin'." He slipped into his room and shut the door.

Staring at the closed door, Moira fumed. She longed to shake some sense into the young hellion, but nothing reached him. Maybe if he found a good woman, she'd tame him. Too bad the local lasses fell under his spell, and he had his way with most of them. Much too soon, he lost interest and looked for new flowers to pluck.

He'd inherited Da's gift of gab and charm, more's the pity. How Mam managed to raise a family and keep Da working, Moira never knew. Eventually he drank one too many whiskeys and passed out on the road one cold winter's night. They carried him home, stiff as a starched sheet. Mam cried for days, but mainly to keep old Fiona satisfied. A year later, the good Lord took her home. Moira always thought Mam died of too much work and too many beatings.

Before she passed, Mam made Moira promise to watch over Ewan and see he didn't end like Da. Despite her constant efforts, her failure to change her brother's ways rankled. She extricated him from one scrape after another, but he always raced off to the next one. He'd become more than she could manage. He needed the hand of a strong man, a man like Connor Kehoe.

So far, Connor had no time for Ewan and avoided him like poison. If Connor married her, he'd have to help curb Ewan. Rory Doyle had asked her, but she didn't love him and couldn't envision him coping with her high-spirited brother. Mild mannered and easygoing, Rory would only try to cajole Ewan into behaving. He always expected others to follow God and atone for their sins. Ewan didn't consider himself a sinner. That he admired Connor while ignoring Rory might be a sign to follow her heart.

Unfortunately, Ewan spent money, always more money, and she found it harder to come by. Despite the export market for her sweaters, business had dropped off far more than expected, and Ewan's expensive hobbies consumed every penny they had. That American car of his had to go. Why he'd leased it in the first place, she had no idea, nor did she know why the leasing company agreed to his terms.

Tomorrow she would make him take the car back. At least that would eliminate one unnecessary expense. With a sigh, Moira returned to her room and slipped into bed. Sleep took its time returning.

* * * *

Mist shrouded the dark landscape and blurred all features. Moira recognized nothing, yet she had seen this place before. It existed nowhere else but in her visions. Breathless, she waited for some sign.

A woe-laden keening filled the air and struck her soul—the *bean sidhe*. What or whom did it mourn? She shuddered and covered her ears, but the grief of the cry intensified. Pulling her shawl tighter, she shivered. The damp air sucked all warmth away.

A large black crow, wings spread wide, swooped low and almost hit her. The bird croaked in a hoarse voice and veered off, skimming her head. The breeze from its passing riffled her hair before the bird faded into the mist.

A tall, illusive shape took form. At first, she couldn't tell what it represented—a man, a woman, or some other creature. The mournful keening increased and almost deafened her. Please, God, not the *bean sidhe*, she prayed, gripping the silver cross she always wore. The mist shredded as the unknown form advanced. Moira squinted, struggling to bring the image into focus.

As the mist shrouding the figure thinned, a dark woman emerged. Clad in a sort of green, and slender as a young alder, she wore a bright gold sun on her breast. From somewhere, a shaft of light flashed from the ornament and almost blinded Moira.

When she opened her eyes, the woman had vanished.

* * * *

Morning sun shone through the casement and woke Moira. She shook her head, struggling with the images in the vision. Had it come as a warning? But of what? She'd never met such a woman before. Too often, her dreams came as warnings, but often the meaning took some unscrambling. Mam had passed along her ability to predict the future sometimes, but the veiled hints in these visions confused her.

She knew no one like this dark stranger, or whether she symbolized good or evil. Only the unfolding events would show the true nature of the vision or whatever the woman symbolized. She prayed it was not the Morrigan come to claim a life.

Despite the crow and the mist, she refused to believe the woman personified evil or death. Black or white might signify death, even blood red, but not the sun or the green clothing this one wore. They gave lie to darkness and death.

Moira could not recall seeing anyone like the woman. Few dark-skinned strangers came to Kilconon. Dublin, Cork, or even Galway might see such people. Eventually, the events related to the vision would unfold and perhaps then, she would understand.

The gold of the sun could signify light, warmth, or even prosperity. Did it portend a change in fortune? With money in short supply, and Ewan's expensive habits, she would welcome any improvement in their prospects. For now, she could only pray the vision meant good fortune.

Musing over the meaning of the images, she noticed Ewan's door remained closed and assumed he slept, oblivious to any noise she might make. Downstairs she made tea, toast, and a boiled egg for breakfast. If he couldn't keep decent hours, he'd have to do for himself.

She should check the Internet for orders and open the shop. There were a few orders to fill and a sweater to finish. A tourist or two might even come.

If only Ewan would settle down. A good woman, babes, and a job would stop his wildness. All she had was patience.

Chapter Four

The next morning Tula rose early and entered the B&B breakfast room at seven. With no idea where her search for her father's origins might lead, she intended to start with the village of Kilconon. Mrs. Kennedy had given her the number of the bus she needed to take, but first, she'd better have the hearty breakfast her hostess offered.

Jerome and Geneva Kelly sat at a table for four by the window. Curtains with yellow roses framed the window while a single yellow rose in a glass vase occupied the middle of their table. Another four tables, all empty, filled the room. A large yellow teapot steamed invitingly on the Kellys' table.

With a smile, Tula joined them. "Good morning. I trust you slept well."

"I did, but Jerome ate and drank too much last night. He groaned the night away."

"Maybe jet-lag complicated things," Tula suggested.

Jerome gave her a thankful smile. "What did I tell you, honeybun? I even remembered to pour the milk in my cup first."

"That you did, but I still say less food and warm beer would have helped."

Mrs. Kennedy entered with two plates and set them before the Kellys. "How about you, Miss Mohr? How do you like your eggs and rashers? Most Americans want the rashers burnt. The tea, toast, jam, and butter are on the table."

Tula couldn't suppress an amused grin. "We call it crisp, but then our bacon is different. Yours is more like Canadian bacon. I'll try it the Irish way."

"Right you are, miss." Mrs. Kennedy bustled off toward the kitchen.

Remembering how strong the Irish liked their tea, Tula followed Jerome's example by pouring milk in the cup, adding tea, and then a little hot water. "You're off sightseeing this morning with Captain Kehoe?"

Geneva nodded. "He wanted us to have a day to adjust before going out on the boat. Said he didn't want us to get seasick. Considering Jerome's condition, I think he's right."

"Now, honeybun, don't get a twist in your knickers."

"Jerome. Where in the world did you pick up that?"

"Some man at the pub said it to his wife. I liked the sound of it." He loaded his fork with egg and a small piece of bacon.

Geneva sighed and looked to Tula. "What we women have to endure."

Mrs. Kennedy returned with Tula's breakfast and set it in front of her. Two beautiful eggs, a half tomato, and a rasher of Irish bacon with the fat warm, but not crisp awaited her. "Enjoy. The Captain will be here at eight."

"We'll be ready," Geneva replied.

Knife in her right hand and fork in the left, tines down, Tula cut the rasher and used the knife to push a piece of fried egg on to the fork as well. Geneva stared at the fork for a moment and then looked away. Tula smiled, but ate before cutting more bacon.

"I went to school in Switzerland, so eating like a European comes natural."

"Oh, I see." Geneva blinked. "Guess we Americans stand out. Everybody wears jeans and tennis shoes now, but the Irish still eat like Europeans."

"Yes, Ireland is part of the European Union, although they favor an English style breakfast, and they call tennis shoes trainers."

"Oh, more things to learn."

"Don't worry about it. The Irish like tourists and their money, although they see a lot of Germans and Scandinavians, as well as Americans." Tula sipped her tea. "Mrs. Kennedy serves a good breakfast."

"Yes, but how did you like the raw bacon? I don't think I could eat it." Geneva shuddered.

"Tasty, actually. Well, I must be off to catch my bus. I plan to visit my father's birthplace today and see if I can locate an odd cousin or two. Enjoy your sightseeing." Tula pushed back from the table and rose.

"Miss Mohr, Mr. and Mrs. Kelly, good mornin'." Captain Kehoe stood in the doorway, his cap in his hands. "It's a pleasure to see you on such a bright morning. Are you ready to visit some sights?"

"Yes, we're ready," Geneva gave him a broad smile. "Come on, Jerome; let's not keep the captain waiting."

"Would you like to join us, Miss Mohr?" His blue eyes sparkled and invited Tula to more than sightseeing.

She returned his smile. "You tempt me, but I plan to visit Kilconon today. I'm hoping to find information on my father, and perhaps a relative or two."

"It's a lovely wee village. You'd best ask at the church first. They keep the birth and death records. The registry office in Dingle probably has copies, but I suspect you'd rather see your father's birthplace."

"Thanks for the advice. I'm off to catch a bus. I hope you have a pleasant day." She started to step forward.

"You know, Miss Mohr, we pass by there on our way to the Cliffs of Moher," Captain Kehoe said. "We could drop you at the church. No inconvenience at all, and save you the bus ride."

Tula was tempted, but hated to take advantage of his generosity. "I'd delay you."

"No delay at all. I'm sure the Kellys don't mind. Right, Mr. Kelly?"

"How could we disagree? We like Miss Mohr," Jerome replied. "Say, Tula, did your name come from those Cliffs?"

"I've no idea. Ask me tonight, I might know then." Tula turned to Captain Kehoe. "I appreciate your offer. I'd be a fool to refuse."

"We'll drop you at the Kil."

"Kill?" Geneva whispered, a shocked look on her plump face.

"Kil, kirk, church," Tula supplied.

"Oh, of course."

They gathered jackets, cameras, and purses, and piled in the van standing by the door. Captain Kehoe's warm touch on Tula's hand lingered in her thoughts. These Irish men had all too much charm, and Captain Kehoe also had all of Mario's suave assurance. She'd better

29

watch herself. She couldn't decide if a fling would help her recovery or end in more hurt. She wasn't one to cling to the past, especially when the present offered interesting opportunities.

A half hour later, the van entered the small village of Kilconon. It looked just like the tourist pictures she had seen online. Surprised and relieved, Tula gazed at the settlement perched on the side of a small stream. Whitewashed stone cottages, some with thatched roofs, lined both banks, and a stone bridge connected the two sides. Captain Kehoe parked before a stone church and opened the van door.

He held out his hand to Tula and the now familiar touch of his fingers made her face glow. She stepped down, reluctant to release his hand.

"Just ask for Dominie Donnelly," Connor said as he closed the van door. "He's sure to know all the families in the parish. Good luck." He tipped his cap with a jaunty smile and returned to the van.

Tula waved as they drove off and the Kellys waved back. Did Connor Kehoe treat all women tourists with the same charming manners? She hoped he didn't and that he meant more, but would she see him again? Maybe she should take one of his tours.

Turning to the church, it looked smaller than she had expected. A little gray walled cottage sat to the right behind a white wooden fence. An abundant garden testified to the rich Irish soil, mild climate, and frequent rain. Pink climbing roses framed the doorway and scented the air. After opening the gate, Tula followed the brick path to the sturdy green door. She knocked and then waited.

Soon the door opened a crack. A gray haired woman stared at her. "It's Father you be wanting?"

"Yes, Father Donnelly. Is he in?"

"He's in his study. And who may you be, miss?"

"I'm Tula Mohr, from Columbus, Ohio."

"A good Irish name. If you wait a moment, I'll tell Father." The plump woman turned and waddled down the short hall to a door at the end and knocked.

Tula gazed about the cozy entry. The housekeeper must be conscientious. A hall tree in dark wood stood to the left, and a matching small table sat next to it below a round mirror on the wall. All the wood gleamed without a speck of dust.

A short man in a black suit with a Roman collar approached. "Miss More? You asked to see me?"

"I'm an American, and like many visitors to Ireland, am looking for my roots. My father, Brendan Mohr, came from Kilconon, and I've come to look for any relatives."

"Your father?" The priest eyed her with a raised eyebrow.

Tula smiled, too used to such reactions to take offence. Her café au lait skin, her Somali mother's legacy, often confused people. "He died some years ago and never mentioned any relatives, but he spoke fondly of his childhood in Kilconon. I decided to see the place for myself and locate anyone who might have known him."

"I see. That's before my time. We can check the church registry and see what we find. If you'll follow me?" He led the way down the hall to the door at the end and opened it.

Inside, shelves filled with books lined three sides of the room and framed a small window. The glow from a grate with a small peat fire in the center of the other wall caught her eye. A large wooden desk with books and papers covering its surface sat nearby. A pleasant place to write a sermon or talk with parishioners.

Father Donnelly sat in the leather chair behind the desk and motioned Tula to one of the small visitor's chairs in front of it. "Do you know the names of your father's parents?"

"No, I don't. He never mentioned them."

He eyed Tula for a moment. "Umm, let's start sixty years ago and see what we find for the Mohrs."

He went to the shelf on the right and looked among a number of leather bound volumes. "Here we go." He pulled a large book from the stack and blew off the dust. "It looks like no one's consulted this for some time."

He carried the heavy book to the desk and began to thumb through the pages. "More was it? M-o-o-re? Moher?"

"No, M-o-h-r."

"Of course. Brendan Mohr?"

"Yes." Tula confirmed the name and smiled.

"Did he have a middle name?"

"He never used one. Let me think.... Brendan.... As I recall, it began with an 'a.' Brendan Adam? No." She shook her head and thought some more. "Brendan Adare Mohr."

He scanned several page. "Ah, here it is. Brendan Adare Mohr born to Deidre Moira Clare and Sean Mohr. We have no Mohrs in the parish now, but we have several Clares. They're probably relatives of your grandmother. In fact, a Moira Clare has a shop in the village next to the grocer. You might talk with her."

His news surprised and pleased her. Maybe she had a relative or two after all. That might make this trip a cause for celebration. A family. The idea intrigued her and she wondered what this Moira Clare would be like.

"Thank you, I'll do that. You've provided the information I needed." Tula opened her wallet. "Will you accept a small donation to the church?"

"We always welcome donations. Kilconon has fallen on hard times of late, and we get few tourists here."

"Traveler's checks okay?"

He smiled, revealing a gold tooth. "Most certainly. The bank welcomes them."

Tula removed a check for a hundred dollars. She signed it and handed it to Father Donnelly. "At least now I know my grandparents' names, and with luck, this Moira Clare can tell me more."

Father Donnelly led her to the cottage door. "We have services on Sunday. We'd like to see you there."

"My plans are uncertain, but I'll keep that in mind."

Tula had not expected such easy success. She doubted the Dingle Registry would have told her about Moira Clare. Walking toward the village center, she wondered about the woman.

She soon reached the crossroads in the center of the village. Stone cottages lined both sides of the road. A combination newsagent, small chemist shop, and post office stood on the left, next to a pub-cum-hotel the sign identified as the Kilconon Arms. On the right, a grocery with green wellies, the tall rubber boots used by farmers, in front and a stack of pitchforks sat next to another small shop. Tula assumed the adjacent shop must belong to Moira Clare.

Despite a large breakfast, her stomach rumbled, reminding her lunchtime had arrived, although the Irish, like the Brits, ate at about one instead of noon. The visit to Moira Clare would be better done when she wasn't hungry. Seeing no restaurant or coffee shop, she entered the pub.

A low peat fire burned in the fireplace. The dim lighting revealed dark tables and chairs clustered around the fireplace and along the wall. Seeing only a barmaid wiping the usual bar, Tula approached her.

"Do you serve tea?"

"We're an Irish pub." The barmaid grinned at her. "Sure now, we have tea."

"I'd like some and… Do you have cut sandwiches?"

"We have the lot—bangers and mash, fish and chips, gammon sandwiches, ploughman's lunch." She pointed to a chalkboard on the wall. "The fish were fresh caught in the morning catch."

"I'll try the fish and chips."

"Have a seat, and I'll bring your tea." The generously endowed barmaid smiled and left through a doorway behind the bar.

Tula walked toward the fireplace and sat in a chair by the low glow of the fire, musing about Kilconon, her grandparents, and the Clares. The village was small and had fallen on hard times, according to Father Donnelly. That didn't bode well for Moira Clare's shop.

The brassy-haired barmaid brought the tea, milk, sugar crystals, and a pot of hot water. "The fish'll be up shortly."

"Thank you. By the way, do you know Moira Clare?"

"Moira? Sure I do. She knits fancy sweaters. Have you come for one?"

"I'm not sure. I didn't know that. I've heard she might have known my father, Brendan Mohr."

"Mohr? None here now, but there's an old cottage down the lane called Mohr Cottage. Can't say, as I knew any Mohrs. Now, the Clares, they're still here, at least Ewan and Moira are."

"Ewan?" Tula recalled the cocky young man at the shop in Dingle. "Does he drive a red sports car?"

"That's Ewan. He likes fast cars and easy women. You'd best watch out for him. He'd charm the knickers off anything in skirts."

"I thought he had a girl in Dingle."

"He has 'em all over the place. Even tried to con me once, but I know better. Poor Moira, she tries to mother him, but he's a wild one." A bell rang. "That's your food." She hurried off toward the serving window and returned with a plate of steaming food. "Enjoy."

Putting aside thought of Moira for the moment, Tula concentrated on the food. The white, flakey fish surprised her. So did the french fries, chips as the Irish and Brits called them. Unlike the frozen type, these tasted like real Irish potatoes. All in all, she congratulated herself on having chosen well for lunch. Replete, she leaned back and enjoyed the rest of the tea.

Sated, she felt able to tackle Moira Clare and discover what she knew of the Mohrs and would share. Anticipation stirred Tula's senses.

Chapter Five

Outside the Kilconon pub, a brisk breeze greeted Tula. Two women entered the grocery store with the pitchforks and wellies in front, but otherwise the street was empty. Most people must be working or busy elsewhere.

Tula walked across the street to Moira Clare's shop and studied the knitted garments displayed in the window—sweaters with scarves, mittens, and hats. The striking sweater in the center featured a large, white sunburst against a black background. The design surprised her. A second one featured a large black bird with wings spread against white. Something about the bird set Tula on edge. A sense of menace she could not identify radiated from it. The designs had a fey quality and lacked any of the traditional Irish embellishments of Celtic knots, twisted cables, or shamrocks used in most Irish knitwear.

Intrigued, she opened the shop door and a bell above it jingled. She entered and saw an attractive, black haired woman, not young, but not yet middle-aged, sitting behind the counter. The woman glanced up from her knitting.

* * * *

Moira stared at the woman entering the shop. Her palms grew sweaty and her pulse raced. It couldn't be. She blinked, but the woman remained. She knew her. She had half expected her to come, but had also hoped never to see the woman from her dream. For a brief moment, her last seeing overlaid the real person. The dark hair like a nimbus surrounding her head, and the dusky skin matched the image. This woman wore the same green garment, but no golden sun hung around her neck.

35

Moira breathed again, as relief brought her back to reality. A blink followed, and her gaze returned to one of a more acceptable blandness suitable to greet a potential customer.

"Can I help you?" she said in her best voice, but she didn't smile.

"I hope so." The woman paused a moment unsure how to begin. "Are you Moira Clare?"

"I am. This is my shop, and I make everything in it." Her voice carried a note of stiff pride.

The strange woman nodded, as if relieved. "Then I've come to the right place. I'd like to see the sweater in the window."

"Which one?"

"The one with the sunburst."

"A bold one, that." Moira rose and walked to the window to remove the sweater. She replaced it with the crow sweater.

With the garment in hand, she returned to the counter and handed it to the customer. "It's made of a fine Irish wool, all natural. It's not dyed. You'll find it's very soft, not like most of the coarser wools used for most Irish sweaters. It's almost as fine as those in the traditional ring shawls."

Nodding, the woman tourist examined the sunburst in detail and then slipped one hand inside. Stroking the outside, she ran a hand over the design. Moira was proud her stitches were even and precise, not like some of the shoddy goods sold in Dingle.

"How much is it?"

Moira eyed the woman from head to toe, assessing what this tourist might pay. "Dollars, Euros, Pounds?"

"Dollars, please."

"You come from the States?"

"Columbus, Ohio," she confirmed.

"O-Hi-O? That's west of Boston. America is a big country."

"It is, and yes, Columbus is south and west of Boston, about eight hundred miles or so. The U.S. is three thousand miles coast to coast."

"Imagine that," Moira replied. "Ireland is but two hundred miles wide, or should I say three hundred-thirty-three kilometres. 'Course, the roads wind a bit and sheep get in the way off the N routes. You asked about the sweater. It's unique, but I've had it awhile." She again studied the tourist considering how much she could expect an American might spend. "A hundred and… fifty, yes, a hundred and fifty dollars."

Pursing her lips, the stranger considered the price.

* * * *

Tula again stroked the sweater. Did she really need another one, even a hand-knit one in a fine wool? She'd come for information, not a sweater. Suspecting she could bargain with this Moira Clare, she rejected that in favor of sweetening her mood. If she paid the price demanded, she would put Moira in her debt.

"Credit cards, traveler's checks?"

"I take them all, but the bank prefers traveler's checks."

Tula pulled out her wallet and removed two checks. At this rate, she'd have to visit a bank soon. She would have to use credit cards for the rest of her trip, with maybe a judicious cash withdrawal as well.

The shopkeeper laid tissue over the sweater, folded it with care, and inserted more tissue between the folds. She then placed it in a box.

Tula handed her the traveler checks, and taking the box, smiled. "This is a pretty village—sort of quaint."

"Umm. It's fallen on hard times. Small villages either grow or disappear. The young leave. Some go to America. There are no jobs here."

"Yet you stay."

Moira snorted in disdain. "Where else could I go? Kilconon is my home."

"My father's too, according to Father Donnelly," Tula said.

"Your name is Mohr?" Moira looked as if she doubted that.

"Yes, my father was Brendan Mohr. Brendan Adare Mohr. My grandmother was Deidre Moira Clare."

Moira's dark eyes narrowed as they surveyed her. "You don't look Irish."

That made Tula laugh. "My father married a Somali woman, so I'm half-Irish. He met my mother in London and they married. I came later. At present, I'm looking for any relatives."

"Where is your father now?" Moira had a speculative gleam in her eyes.

"He and my mother died while I was in college."

"Sorry I am to hear that." Moira paused, studying her, and then continued. "As a wee one, I remember when Brendan left. It broke his mam's heart, and she died soon after."

Tula did not believe her father would have been that forgetful or cruel. "How sad. He never mentioned that. I wonder if he knew. My mother came from a wealthy family, and they traveled a lot."

Moira quirked an eyebrow. "You're an heiress then?"

Tula sniffed, amused that foreigners always assumed that. "I'm solvent. I own a small café in Columbus. I'm a shopkeeper like you."

"A business woman." Moira nodded and a warm smile followed. "Well, pleased I am to meet you, Cousin." She held out her hand and clasped Tula's.

The icy touch and the strength of Moira's fingers surprised Tula. All that knitting made them supple. She returned a brief squeeze in acknowledgement of the greeting. A real Irish cousin.

"My brother Ewan and I are the last of the Clares, so it's good you've come. How long do you plan to stay?"

Relieved and happy at Moira's positive reception of her, Tula had no idea of a possible return date. She had booked a three-week return ticket. "I hadn't planned that far yet. Now that I've found you, I'll stay at least a week or so. I want to spend some time here in Kilconon, and maybe visit the old cottage the barmaid mentioned—Mohr Cottage."

"I suspect Jenny told you it's derelict and falling to ruin." Moira shook her head. "Not a fit place to stay."

"There's the Kilconon Arms, unless there's a B&B nearby?"

Moira looked thoughtful for a moment. "I've a better idea, Cousin. You can stay with Ewan and me."

"We've only just met. I'd hate to impose." Maybe they wouldn't like one another once they spent time together. Practicality said yes, but commonsense cautioned.

"I insist. You'd do the same for me if I visited O-hi-o. Consider it settled. Where are you staying now?"

"I'm at Mrs. Kennedy's B&B near Dingle."

"I'll ring and tell her. My brother, Ewan, can pick up your luggage. He'll be pleased to meet you."

"Ewan?" The image of the brash young man she and Geneva saw in Dingle rose in her mind and the barmaid had confirmed it. "Does he drive a red Dodge Viper?"

"Ah, you've met him?" Moira smiled.

"In a way. I saw him flirting with the clerk in the Dingle jewelry shop." She neglected to mention his tailgating Connor's van.

"That's Ewan. He has an eye for the ladies." Moira sighed. "Would you care for a cuppa?"

"I had tea a bit ago, but I'd love one now."

"With so few folks about and no tourist buses scheduled, I'll close the shop, and we can go to the cottage." Moira put away her knitting and turned the sign on the door.

Outside, the sunshine brightened the landscape. The trees and grassy fields beyond the villages glowed in a variety of vibrant greens. The houses with gardens had colorful flowers that delighted the eyes with reds, pink, yellow, orange, and some blue, giving them a festive air. The scent of roses overlaid the air.

Moira led the way at a brisk walk along the lane. In ten minutes, they reached a thatched, grey stone cottage nestled in a lush garden. It resembled a fairytale dwelling in the midst of vivid flowers and greenery.

"The Clares have lived here for two hundred years or more." After opening a rusty iron gate, she walked along the flagstone path to the house. "My people kept adding to it as the family and their means grew. With just Ewan and I left, it's a bit too large."

Moira opened the faded red door and held it for Tula. "We seldom use the dining room or the two spare bedrooms. Ewan and I are very informal and eat in the kitchen."

Inside, Tula noted the beautiful dark wood wardrobe beside the door. Most likely Victorian. The tidy living room contained comfortable looking chintz armchairs and a sofa. Everything looked a bit dated, as if time stopped here years before. However, a small electric fire occupied the fireplace. From the appearance of the place, Tula guessed the knitted-wear business brought in enough to support the Clares, but not to change or update things.

Moira led the way to the kitchen. It looked more recent with a small, modern fridge and gas stove. Tula liked the cream-colored walls and black linoleum on the floor. A large pine table had four ladder-backed chairs with rush seats like the ones she'd bought for her cafe. Perhaps she'd inherited her liking for them from her father. The room appeared immaculate.

"Sit down while I fill the kettle," Moira said from where she stood at the sink.

Pulling out a chair, Tula sat and gazed toward the small window over the sink. Green ivy framed the outside of the window and herb pots on glass shelves took advantage of the light. Moira bustled about gathering cups, saucers, a milk jug, and spoons. A flowered patterned sugar bowl already sat on the table and stood out in contrast to the surroundings of cream and black.

"I'll see if Ewan's here." Moira turned on the heat under the kettle and walked toward stairs just visible to the left beyond the doorway.

To learn the names of her grandparents, and discover she even had living cousins, came as an unexpected and pleasant surprise to Tula. That Moira had known her father amazed her even more. She had thought Moira close to her own age, but if she remembered Brendan, she must be five or six years older. Having grown used to being the sole surviving Mohr, she had given up all hope of relatives. Now she had not one, but two cousins, even if one of them was an Irish rogue.

* * * *

Moira hurried up the stairs and prayed Ewan hadn't gone yet. She banged on his door. "Ewan, Ewan, are you there?"

A groan sounded. "Go away, I'm sleeping."

"Wake up, sleepyhead. We have company. An American cousin is here."

"Cousin? Sure now, we don't have any cousins."

Moira leaned close to the door. She didn't want the American woman to hear her. "Get dressed and come downstairs. I'm fixing tea. And Ewan, she has money."

"A cousin with money?"

"Shh, not so loud. Get dressed, and you can meet her." Moira spun on her heel and hurried downstairs.

The whistle of the teakettle greeted her as she entered the kitchen. "I'll have tea in a trice." She rinsed the black teapot with boiling water, added a good measure of tea, and filled it. "Ewan will join us." Covering the pot with knitted cozy having the shape of rooster, she then carried it to the table.

Tula smiled at her. "When Ewan comes, you can introduce us. From what I observed, he kissed the Blarney Stone."

"Sure now, no Clare needs to do that. They're born with Irish charm. In Ewan's case, too much so." Moira sighed.

She filled the milk jug and set a plate of currant scones before Tula. "Ah, here's the man himself."

Tula looked toward the doorway and smiled as Ewan entered. "Cousin Ewan, we passed in the Dingle jewelry store yesterday."

Moira noticed his recognition of the Mohr woman, and he glanced at Moira, his eyes filled with questions.

"Tula comes from O-hi-o. Our uncle… Brendan Mohr was her Da. You may not remember him. I think Mam had you after he left."

"Ah, I remember you well." With an intense look, Ewan took Tula's hand and kissed it. "An older bird… lady, with you."

"Geneva Kelly. Yes, we were looking in the shops before dinner. We'd just arrived from the States. You seemed rather taken with the pretty clerk."

"She's a lively piece. We went dancing later. Moira says you're our cousin."

"That's what Father Donnelly told me, too. I'd no idea any relatives still lived here."

"It's our good fortune you've come," Ewan said and followed his words with a crooked grin.

Moira shook her head. Ewan had best watch himself. "I've asked Tula to stay with us while she's in Kilconon. You'll have to bring her luggage from Mrs. Kennedy's B&B in Dingle."

"At your service." Ewan saluted and bowed. "When?"

"Have some tea first, and we'll work that out," Moira replied and turned to Tula. "I baked the scones fresh this morning and I made the jam with the berries out back."

Tula nodded, lathered a scone with butter and jam, and took a bite.

"Moira, these are delicious. I make scones for my café, but these are better, and the jam is superb. Maybe I can import some from you."

Moira laughed at the suggestion. "Take a jar home, but as to export/import, the EU regulations are too costly and cumbersome. You can have plenty of the jam and scones by staying right here in Kilconon."

"At least for the duration of my trip." Tula broke open another scone. "There's so much to learn about Ireland and my father. Moira, can you tell me the family history?"

"There's little to tell. We're not famous. There are no heroes or noblemen in the family tree. Canada and America took our best." Moira sighed and poured a cup of tea. "At least you've found the last of us."

"Yes, my roots and more. Family." Tula bit into the second scone.

To Moira, Tula looked happy. A good sign. Moira pondered what course to follow. As yet, she had no idea how her visions related to the future. They had forewarned her of her cousin's arrival, but had they no greater meaning? Yet that didn't explain the *bean sidhe*.

Moira suppressed a shiver of fear. As she sipped her tea, she looked from Tula to Ewan and mulled over what the future held for the three of them.

Chapter Six

In the cottage drive, Ewan held the door of the Viper for Tula so she could slide into the red roadster. She fastened a silk scarf around her head, certain the speed of his driving would otherwise leave her hair in a tangled mess.

"Have you much luggage, Cousin?" Ewan put the car in gear and roared onto the road.

Acceleration pressed Tula against the seatback. "No. One small carry-on and a small bag is all."

"Travel light do you?"

"Mostly. I learned years ago to never pack more than I can carry."

"Most tourists I meet bring too many cases. This car lacks space, but we can manage yours all right. If it doesn't fit, I'll bring you back and get it later."

He shifted gears and the scenery vanished in a blur of motion. He took every curve at top speed and only braked once for a string of cows crossing the road. Barred metal gates provided access to the pastureland while high hedges hid much of the scenery beyond the narrow roadway.

Almost immediately ahead, a herd of cows spilled across the road dropping dung as they crossed. Ewan hit the brakes, throwing Tula forward, and stopped with a squeal just inches from a cow. He drummed his fingers on the steering wheel. Tula considered herself lucky she had braced herself and was only thrown against the windshield instead of through it.

"Sure now, they ought to keep the cattle off the roads," Ewan muttered.

"Maybe you should drive a little slower," she responded drily.

"Ah, Cousin, that would take all the sport out of driving." He grinned at her, shifted gears, and took off with a roar, almost hitting the trailing cow.

They made it to Mrs. Kennedy's in fifteen minutes. Moira had called ahead, and Mrs. Kennedy waited for them by the door.

"Sorry I am, you're leaving, Miss Mohr."

"I am too," Tula responded, "but I can't refuse my cousins."

"No, 'course you can't. If you need a place in Dingle again, remember us."

"I will. You have a lovely place." Tula opened her purse. "I owe you for two nights. Do you take credit cards?"

"Yes, MasterCard or Visa. You don't need to pay the second night."

"Look on it as payment for the inconvenience." Tula handed her a credit card. "I'll just get my things while you enter the charge."

She hurried down the hall to her room and retrieved her bag. A quick check revealed no stray garments anywhere. She added her toiletries kit to the smallish bag and carried it to the entrance. Mrs. Kennedy handed her a slip to sign and her card. Finished, Tula handed the bag to Ewan, who stowed it in the Viper.

"Now, Cousin, time for a pint at the pub." Ewan grinned at her with a wink. "Driving these dusty roads is thirsty work."

"Only if it won't impair your driving." Tula eyed him with a smidgen of distrust. "In that case, I'll drive. I've always wanted to try one of these high-powered cars."

"Don't you know drink is mother's milk to an Irishman?"

"Here I thought it was whiskey. Anyway, I'll make mine tea. One of us needs to remain sober."

Ewan drove into the Dingle town center and parked at the nearest pub. Inside, he seated Tula at a banquette near the fireplace and went to the bar. The smell of beer almost overwhelmed her as she glanced around the cozy interior and wondered yet again, why pubs used somber colors and low lighting. The peat fire in the hearth glowed with warmth and provided the little light.

Even the upholstered seats of the wooden chairs were covered in dark green leatherette. Small stools stained almost black added more seating, while matching tables provided a place for drinks. The late afternoon clientele consisted of a few men lounging at the bar and chatting to the black-haired barmaid.

Ewan soon returned with a brimming glass. "Welcome, Cousin," he said sliding onto the bench next to her. "Brig'll bring your tea. Glad I am you've come to us. Moira and I thought we had no family, and from America yet."

Tula nodded. "I thought the same. After my parents died, I gave up hope of locating any relatives."

He took her hand in his and fixed his dark, soulful eyes on her. "Now you've found the two of us. Moira likes you. She always wanted a sister instead of a rake of a brother." He grinned at her with a twinkle in his espresso eyes.

Plump, curly-haired Brig appeared with a cup, teapot, and fixings. Tula thanked her before turning to Ewan.

She had seen him with the jewelry store clerk and doubted that he had any real interest in her. "I like Moira. She's articulate and talented. I love the fine craftsmanship and unique designs in her sweaters."

"Indeed, she sells them all over the world." Ewan edged closer until his hip nudged hers. "With you staying at the cottage, I'll take you to see all the sights. Maybe you'd like to go to a *ceili*?"

"A what?" Tula stared at him.

He grinned back. "A night to remember of Irish music, dance, and plenty of spirits. I guarantee you a good time, Cousin." He squeezed her hand while his crooked grin and dancing eyes promised just that and more.

The door of the pub opened and a familiar group of three entered. She recognized the Kellys and Captain Kehoe. They looked around the room and spotted her.

"Tula," Geneva gushed. "I see you've met the Viper owner." She gave Ewan a coy smile. "May we join you?"

"Of course." Tula smiled at her, amused at Geneva's all too obvious assumptions about Ewan. "Hello, Jerome, Captain Kehoe."

"Miss Mohr." The captain tipped his cap to her and frowned at Ewan.

"Hi," Jerome added and sat in a chair across from Tula. "Those cliffs are something. Not so spectacular as the Grand Canyon, but pretty impressive."

"He means the Cliffs of Moher," Geneva whispered. "I thought of you since your name sounds the same."

"I'll just step to the bar for the drinks," Captain Kehoe said. "What's your pleasure?"

"A Guinness for me," Jerome responded, which made Geneva shudder.

"A cider please," she responded.

"We make the best cider in Ireland," Connor said. "Anything for you Miss Mohr?" Tula shook her head.

When Captain Kehoe departed, she turned to Geneva. "No, not the Cliffs. Maybe at some point the family had some tie to them, but we spell ours without the 'e.' Jerome, Geneva, this is my cousin, Ewan Clare."

"Cousin?" Wide-eyed, Geneva stared from Tula to Ewan and back.

"Yes, well, sort of. His grandfather and my Irish grandmother came from the same family. Ewan has a sister too, Moira."

"How wonderful for you. Cousins. You never said anything about that." Geneva looked both disappointed and avid for more.

Grinning, Tula took pity on her. "I only just found out myself. I'm the last Mohr and Ewan and Moira are the last Clares."

"And lucky we are to find such a treasure." Ewan lifted Tula's hand and kissed it.

"I see he's kissed the Blarney Stone," Jerome observed.

"Ah no, I tell the absolute truth. We Irish value family above all. Besides, it's not everyone who can claim such a beauty." He squeezed Tula's hand still clasped in his.

"None of that now." Tula disengaged her hand from his. "I'm staying with Moira for a few days so we can exchange information about our parents and Kilconon."

"Sorry I am to hear that," Captain Kehoe said as he placed glasses before the Kellys. "I hoped you might come with us for a short cruise. We'll be going out tomorrow to see the birds and any migrating whales."

"That sounds wonderful." She clapped her hands and turned to the Kellys. "Would you mind if I joined you?"

"I'd love it," Geneva said. Jerome nodded his approval.

"Good." Captain Kehoe smiled at her before taking a sip of his pint.

"I'll pick you up at Moira's at seven-thirty, and the Kellys at eight."

Frowning, Ewan slid off the banquette and got to his feet. "We must go, Cousin Tula. Moira has our dinner waiting."

"Oh, I hadn't realized how late it was," Tula replied. "I'll say goodbye and see you all tomorrow." She kissed Geneva on the cheek and nodded to the two men who smiled back.

Once they reached the car, Ewan leaned close as he seated her in the Viper. "That's a lovely scent, Cousin." His warm breath caressed her cheek.

She edged away. "Moira's waiting."

He signed and closed the door. "Indeed, but we'll be there in no time, no time at all." He jumped into his seat, put the car into gear, and peeled off with his usual abandon.

Gasping, Tula grabbed the armrest and dug in her fingers. Her knuckles showed white.

The return trip to Kilconon mirrored their earlier breakneck pace. When Ewan missed an old man by inches, Tula hissed. She looked back to see how the man fared and saw him shaking his walking stick at their dust trail.

"Ewan, slow down. You almost hit that man."

"These farmers think they own the roads," he sputtered. "Roads are for cars."

At that moment, a large truck hove into sight. "Ewan, STOP!"

He swung the wheel hard. The car spun and then righted itself to end at a gated entrance to a pasture. The truck whistled past.

Tula released a pent up breath. "That's it. I'll drive."

"Yanks drive on the wrong side of the road. Don't worry, Cousin. I'll get you home. No need to worry about this one." He patted the dash.

"It's not the car; it's the driver," she snapped.

Ewan shifted gears and spun his wheels as the tires took to the road again. Ten breathless minutes later, he parked behind Moira's cottage.

"See? Home with nary a scratch."

Tula's knees threatened to buckle, but she managed to walk unaided to the door.

Moira threw it open. "I expected you an hour ago."

"We had to stop for a lorry." Ewan grinned at her and then took

Tula's bags upstairs.

When Ewan disappeared, Tula turned to her cousin. "Moira, I won't ride with Ewan again. He's an accident waiting to happen."

"I can't say as I blame you. You know young men and fast cars."

"Wrecking the car and killing himself is one thing, but he almost hit an old man. He's a danger to anything in his way."

"I know." Moira sighed. "Dinner's ready—a lovely Irish stew. Come and eat."

Ewan joined them, and they adjourned to the kitchen. Plates of Irish stew, soda bread, and yellow butter comprised the meal. The rich stew and tasty bread testified to Moira's culinary abilities.

Tula savored every bite. "Moira, you have to share this recipe with me."

"Sure now, the Clares can match the best," Ewan said.

Moira gave her a broad smile. "My mam used to make it. So, what do you want to do tomorrow?"

"Captain Kehoe and my friends, the Kellys, asked me to join them on their bird and whale watching trip. The captain will pick me up at seven-thirty, so I hope that's all right with you. I'm not sure what time we'll return."

"In time for dinner, I'm sure. The weather promises fair." Moira looked down at her plate. "I didn't know you knew Connor."

"I rode with him and the Kellys to Dingle, and he recommended Mrs. Kennedy's."

Moira looked thoughtful and nodded. "He grew up in Kilconon, but left for the university. He came back last year and started his boat trips. It's been a hard go for him."

"Don't waste sympathy on him, Moira," Ewan snapped. "He refused to carry a wee bit of cargo for me."

"Cargo?" Moira stared at him with gimlet eyes. "What kind of cargo, Ewan?"

"Just a wee package or two. Takes no room, no room t'all." He glanced at Tula and back to Moira. Clearly unhappy, she said nothing more.

Chapter Seven

Bright sunshine woke Tula the next morning. She squinted at the unfamiliar surroundings until recognition of the room clicked into place—Moira's cottage. Satisfied, she relaxed. She had no desire to rise. Adjusting to the time change was more difficult than she expected.

Yawning, she stretched and checked her watch to see the time—not yet six. She rolled over and tried to sleep, then suddenly remembered today was the boat trip to see the seabirds with the Kellys and the interesting Captain Kehoe. She wondered if he was as pleasant to all the ladies. It might get him more customers. Lots of wealthy widows traveled to Ireland.

Dressed for the boat trip, she started down the stairs. She had no desire to wake her cousins and tested each step as she descended. However, when she reached the sunny kitchen, Moira sat at the table drinking tea. At Tula's entrance, she looked up and smiled. There was no sign of Ewan. Most likely, he'd had a late night and would not be up this early.

"Good morning," Tula greeted her. "I didn't expect to find you awake yet." She took the chair opposite Moira.

"I'm an early riser, not like Ewan, who sleeps late. I 'spect you'd like something to eat. That boat trip will take a few hours. Tea's in the pot on the table. Eggs and a rasher all right?" Moira called over shoulder.

"Sounds fine." Tula savored the strong, dark Irish tea suitably diluted with the rich milk. She added a generous spoon of the sugar crystals and sipped the hot liquid, glad for the warmth.

"At home, sometimes I just settle for tea and toast, but I'm getting used to Irish breakfasts. Besides, who knows where or when lunch will be."

49

"Most likely there's a café or some such on the island," Moira said while she sliced the loaf of dark bread and stuck two pieces in the toaster. "Connor would have told you if there were no food places."

She busied herself at the stove with a fry pan. The aroma of cooking bacon filled the air and raised hunger pangs in Tula. Soon Moira set a full plate of sunny eggs and bacon before her.

Tula buttered the dark bread, seasoned the eggs, and started to eat. The rich Irish butter on the nutty toast added an extra fillip to the eggs. The dark Irish bread was moister and tastier than the packaged varieties sold at home. Too, she was certain it had no preservatives.

At the stove, Moira made a new pot of tea. "I'm sure Connor will serve tea on the trip. I could cut you a sandwich if you like."

Tula considered that and then nodded. "It wouldn't hurt." She poured another cup of tea and leaned back. "Thanks for the delicious breakfast. I enjoyed it. That'll hold me for a while."

"Don't be too sure," Moira said, grinning. "Sea air whets the appetite."

She removed the dishes and replaced the teapot on the table with the fresh one. "Be sure to take a mac. If you don't have one, I'll lend you mine. Sometimes it mists or even rains, and the boat throws up spray if the sea is choppy."

Tula nodded. "I've been on ferries and sailing boats before. I've always enjoyed those trips, so I'm sure I'll like this one. It isn't every day I visit seabird nesting sites or see whales."

"Aye, I limit myself to watching the gulls from the beach these days," Moira said. "There's a nice path to it if you're interested. However, we don't get the puffins or skuas around here. I wonder Ewan isn't going too."

Tula remembered the captain hadn't been happy when Ewan tailgated the van on their arrival in Dingle. Then, last night in the pub, Captain Kehoe had given her cousin a disapproving frown.

"I have the impression he and Captain Kehoe don't like one another."

"No, no," Moira objected. "They've known each other since we were all children together. It's true they don't agree on all things, but I've never heard cross words between them."

Moira busied herself with the dishes and then sandwich making. Finished, she handed a small packet to Tula, who thanked her. "Have you decided what else in Ireland you want to explore?"

"No, not yet. I guess the Cliffs of Moher. The Kellys raved about them and the Burren. I really came to see Kilconon."

"The Cliffs and the Burren are both lovely sights. Ewan could take you any time, but I hope you'll stay with us here in Kilconon a bit and not hurry away. It's not every day we find a cousin."

"Nor I. I'd no idea you and Ewan existed. It's made my trip. I'd also want to see Mohr Cottage. I heard it's a ruin, but I still want to see it."

Moira sighed as if not too pleased. "We can do that tomorrow if you like."

Tula finished her tea and checked her watch. "I should get organized before Captain Kehoe comes." Aware some women didn't welcome others doing chores, she debated whether to offer her help or not. "Can I help wash the dishes?"

"No need. You concentrate on the trip. I'm guessing Connor'll have you home in time for supper. I thought we might have salmon, that is, if you like it."

"I love it. Almost any fish is a favorite of mine. I definitely enjoyed the Irish fish and chips served at the Kilconon Arms. In the States, we eat too much beef."

"I can't promise you a fancy meal, but we never lack for enough to eat." Moira turned to the sink and began to wash the teacups.

Tula hurried upstairs to gather her things. By the time she returned to the kitchen, Captain Kehoe stood talking with her cousin, a mug of tea in his hand. "Morning, Miss Mohr. Ready for our trip?"

"Yes, is there anything special I need?"

"Comfortable shoes, a warm jumper, and a mac. A bottle of water wouldn't go amiss."

"A jumper? Oh, a sweater. Yes, I've one in my pack, a warm one. Moira mentioned the raincoat."

"Right then. We'll see you later, Moira."

"Be sure you bring her back for tea."

"Of course. Shall we go?" He handed Moira his mug and ushered Tula to the door. "You can sit upfront if you like."

She debated whether to read more into that than he meant. The view was better and they could talk more easily. When they reached the van, he held the door for her and helped her into to it. His touch raised anticipation over interesting possibilities, but common sense reminded her the Kellys would soon join them. Then, she again began cynically to wonder if Captain Kehoe affected all his female customers that way. It might help attract more clients, especially the middle-aged widows or single ones.

The drive to Mrs. Kennedy's took a little longer and passed at a more reasonable pace than Ewan's frenzied driving. Neither of them said anything at first as Tula tried to concentrate on the scenery instead of the driver. Green fields and tall, thick fuchsia hedges bordered the road. She'd never seen fuchsia in other than hanging baskets at home. Here, the almost impenetrable bushes of it lined the roadways and formed a formidable barrier. Behind them, low stone walls separated the fields while dairy cows and sheep dotted the lush pastures.

"How do you find the Clares?" Captain Kehoe said, startling her.

"I like Moira a lot, but Ewan… I'm not sure yet. Spoiled?"

"Indeed, he's all that. Moira mothers him too much. Jobs are few, but he could work on the fishing boats, or even for one of the farmers. He's not one to dirty his hands."

His words and the tone of his voice confirmed Tula's opinion of her cousin. "I've asked Moira to take me to Mohr Cottage tomorrow. Do you know it?"

"Indeed, it's derelict at present. A small stone cottage with a thatched roof, but the roof's partially fallen. The walls look solid, but I can't say much else. Some estate agent has it and hasn't found any takers."

At that point, he parked the van in front of Mrs. Kennedy's and hopped out. "I'll just collect the Kellys." In a few minutes, he returned with Jerome and Geneva.

"Hi, Tula, I'm so glad you're going with us," Geneva said as she settled herself next to Jerome in the backseat.

"Me too," Tula replied and smiled warmly. Geneva was such a nice person, and Jerome was amusing and endearing.

In less than ten minutes, Captain Kehoe parked the van near the

52

Dingle waterfront. "I'd suggest you all visit the public toilets before we board. Some people find the head hard to work. I'll be back in ten with the boat." He hurried off toward the pier.

"Head?" Geneva stared at Tula with a puzzled frown.

"That's what they call the toilet on a boat." Tula grinned at her. "I've heard they have a mind of their own."

After a visit to the public toilets, the Kellys and Tula strolled toward the dock. Jerome pulled out a camera and began snapping pictures. A motor launch with a small cabin approached the dock. As it neared, Tula could see Captain Kehoe in the wheelhouse. The *Seabird* was a stubby boat, roughly forty or so feet long with a broad beam and cushioned seats in the open stern. The bright blue hull contrasted with the white wheelhouse and looked suitably nautical.

When almost to the dock, Captain Kehoe darted from the wheelhouse to toss a line to a man waiting at the dock. Once the two men secured the launch, Captain Kehoe shut off the engine and hopped ashore.

Three other people, tall, blond tourists, stood nearby—a man, woman, and a teenage boy. Tula guessed them to be Scandinavians. Captain Kehoe smiled as he approached them.

"If you'll climb aboard the *Seabird*, we'll start our trip. We've fine weather today and should have a smooth voyage."

The Scandinavians and Tula, with Geneva and Jerome, approached the waiting boat. Captain Kehoe pointed out where to place their feet as he helped them board. The three, long-limbed strangers jumped aboard with little or no assistance. Tula's long legs made it easy for her, but Geneva had more trouble. With the help of Captain Kehoe, Jerome, and Tula, she managed to scramble aboard at last. She plumped down next to Tula in the open stern with a relieved sigh.

Despite the mild temperatures the day promised, Tula pulled out the sweater she had bought from Moira and donned it. She fastened a scarf over her hair and slipped on her raincoat.

Geneva gave her a quizzical look. "Are you expecting rain?"

"No, but it's always colder on the water. If it gets too warm, I can take off something. You may be glad you have that windbreaker." The boat moved away from the dock and out into the bay.

"Jerome and Captain Kehoe insisted. Now tell me all about your Irish cousins."

"I only met them both yesterday, so there's little to tell. Moira's a great cook, and she knits striking sweaters, like this one, that she sells online."

"It's beautiful, but I prefer more color." Geneva fingered the sleeve. "My, it's so soft."

"Indeed. I couldn't resist it. Now, I'm even gladder I bought it. Even if we have rain, it'll keep me warm. Can't beat Irish wool for warmth."

"What about your other cousin?"

"You've seen Ewan." Tula grimaced. "He's the Viper driver."

"Oh. Well, he's a dreamboat, although much too young for me. I love those Irish men with the dark hair and eyes. And those brogues…"

"He's handsome all right, but too cocky. I've no objection to him as a cousin, except he's arrogant and drives too fast."

"What else do you do with a car like that? Did they actually know your father?"

"Moira says she has memories of him leaving, but Ewan hadn't even been born then. The Mohrs died out, and Moira and Ewan are the last Clares. Sad in a way, but I'm glad to have found them. My mother's family died out too."

"It must be lonely for you. Jerome has brothers, sisters, aunts, uncles, and almost an entire village of cousins. I've sisters and nieces and nephews." Geneva giggled.

"With my friends and my business, I never lack for things to do," Tula said. "However, this is the first vacation I've taken in years." She sighed over the missed opportunities.

Geneva patted her arm. "I'm glad you're here now. Sightseeing is fun, but it's nicer to share shopping and browsing with another woman. Sometimes a couple becomes too insular. I've mulled over taking some courses in accounting at the local college. Jerome handles all our finances. I figured it wouldn't hurt to learn about money."

"It never does. Too many widows have no idea where the money goes, but you should also consider doing something just for fun, like painting or music."

Sighing, Geneva looked unconvinced and glanced at her husband busy snapping pictures. "I'm not sure Jerome would like it."

Tula sniffed. "He could always take classes too. I'm sure they have some on photography or other subjects he might like." She wondered how many pictures he planned to take of the open sea.

"Jerome, you might want to save some film for the seabirds," she cautioned.

"No worry with this baby. I've got a large storage chip. Anyway, I can always delete some and take new ones. Now, you two hold still and cuddle a little closer."

He backed up and began to focus his shot. Tula edged closer to Geneva and they both smiled. Next, he turned to the Scandinavians, but they waved him off and looked seaward.

The boat rode the waves without any abrupt pitching, and the relatively smooth water made for an easy voyage. When they passed a speedboat, the wake added a bit of chop, but Connor angled the *Seabird* to avoid the worst of the wash. He proved he was a competent sailor.

Tula savored the salt tang, the deep blue of the restless water, and the almost cloudless sky. An hour passed and the coast behind them faded to a dark smudge on the horizon. The three Europeans chatted in some language, most likely Swedish. Tula debated introducing herself, but didn't. Some Europeans were touchy. She had never learned any of the Nordic languages, and the three hadn't spoken any English, although she suspected they understood it.

Then, Connor approached the stern with a large metal teapot. "Tea time. Mugs and fixings are in the center pedestal."

He set the pot down on the deck and fiddled with the wooden pillar in the center of the open stern. He raised shelves around three sides, fastened them in place, and set out mugs and small plastic canisters. A small ledge prevented the mugs from sliding off.

Tula took a mug and added milk powder and sugar. Connor smiled at her and poured it three quarters full with strong tea. Geneva followed suit, as did the others.

Blowing over her mug, Tula sipped cautiously. The hot liquid almost burned her tongue, but she continued to blow over the mug, and it soon reached a comfortable temperature. The Europeans had no problems with the hot tea, but Geneva followed Tula's example and waited for it to cool.

"We'll arrive soon," Connor said and pointed to the dark line dead ahead on the horizon. "Once we land, you can explore the island at your leisure. You'll find a small café near the dock with cut sandwiches, tea and coffee, souvenirs, and a brochure with marked paths to various sites.

"Abandoned cottages lie in the hills, but best avoid them because the roofs have fallen and the places are unstable. Sheep graze there as well. The seabirds roost in the cliffs above, but please watch your footing. Rabbit warrens and bird nests in the ground can trip the unwary. There's no doctor on the island."

"Are there any guides?" Jerome looked hopeful.

"No, but the map in the brochure is easy to follow. The trail is well marked, and the island is small. Once we dock, you'll have three hours to have lunch, shop, explore the island, and check out the birds nesting in the cliffs. Please be at the boat by three-thirty so we can reach Dingle in time for dinner."

When everyone had emptied their mugs, Captain Kehoe collected them and carried them and the teapot into the cabin. He returned shortly to stow the pedestal trays and clear the stern area to make it ready for docking. Above, a few gray clouds loomed on the horizon.

* * * *

Moira walked to the cliff above the shore and perched on a large boulder there. The restless sea splashed over the dark, rocky spines below and then rushed on toward the shingle. So far, she had made little headway with either Ewan or Tula. Both had a streak of Irish stubbornness, but plenty of time remained.

Marriage between them offered a solution to all her problems. She had hopes of convincing Ewan because he needed money. However, Tula had taken a dislike to him. Why couldn't she see how much good he had? He'd make an ideal husband. With her money, all things looked possible for the Clares.

It wasn't as if Ewan could have any rivals. Yet Moira began to fear her new cousin's affections lay elsewhere. She'd made no mention of any American sweetheart, and couldn't have met many Irish men. Only Connor, as far as Moira knew. Connor could use money for his boat. A canny businessman, he must have designs on her cousin and her fortune.

Slate grey clouds blew toward the land, and the sharp wind chilled Moira. She stared into the sky seeking guidance. A haze rose from the water and hid the shingle from view.

The veil of white mist swirled, stirred, but the wind did not dissipate it. Faint images began to emerge. Moira strained to grasp the vision before her. She could just make out a tall, willowy shape and a stockier companion. She tried to see more, but the images remained vague. She thought one might be a woman, but whom? The other grew a bit more solid, not easy to see, but familiar.

The wind had died and the mist figures grew clearer, but remained tantalizing vague, yet somehow almost recognizable. She could swear one of them was Ewan. She heard no voices, but sensed the tall, slender figure was laughing. Then the Ewan one raised his hand as if to hit the woman, but let it fall and stomped away to disappear in the mist leaving the woman alone.

Moira wondered if this was a true seeing of the future, or merely her own thoughts. She narrowed her eyes to peer at the mist woman. The only tall woman she knew was her cousin, Tula. If it was she, it boded ill for Ewan's chances of winning her.

As Moira struggled to make some sense of the vision, a tall, manly figure emerged and approached the mist Tula. Moira watched, held fast. A flicker of fear struck her heart.

The vision grew sharper and more realistic. Connor. It was he who pulled the willowy woman toward him. His arms encircled her, and she put her arms about his neck.

"No," Moira moaned. "NO."

The wind howled and blew all away. Waves washed the empty shore.

Chapter Eight

Mid-morning Moira looked at the kitchen clock yet again. Almost ten and still Ewan hadn't appeared. She put the kettle on to make fresh tea and started toward the stairs. If she didn't rout him out, no telling when he'd show.

She had no more then stepped on first tread when she met him coming down. He yawned and stretched as he descended. "Morning, darlin'," he said as he sat at the table.

"I need to talk with you. Tula's gone out on the *Seabird* with Connor Kehoe this morning." Moira rinsed the teapot with boiling water, added the tea, and filled the pot. She put it in front of Ewan, along with a plate of scones. "Eggs?"

"Yes, and make it two rashers. I'm hungry this morning." He split and buttered a scone.

"You'd best watch out for Connor. He's an eye for the main chance. If he marries her, we'll lose out."

"What woman would take him over me? I'm younger and all the young ones prefer me. Besides, why hurry? They won't be back until evening."

Moira broke the eggs into the pan and turned the rashers. "We need money, and she has it. If you married her, we'd be set."

"Sure now, I could, but why tie on the bag? I'm too young to settle yet." He poured his tea and sipped it.

Moira slammed a plate in front of him. "Look, I canna keep up with you. That car has to go."

"No." He cut the rasher, added a morsel of egg, and chewed with deliberation.

Fuming, Moira sat opposite him and poured a cup of tea. She took a deep breath before speaking. "Marry Tula and let her keep you."

He continued to chew his food and then poured another cup of tea. "Money has its attractions." He grinned at Moira with a raised eyebrow. "You fear she'll take Connor. Jealous, are you?"

"Arghh, there's no talking to you. Leave Connor out of it. If you won't listen and convince Tula, there's no hope for us."

"What if she turns me down?"

"Use that Irish charm you're so proud of. She's a woman and lonely. The perfect target for you, but perhaps you'd rather work for Rory, or even Connor. You live off me, so why not Tula?"

"She's American and…" Ewan rubbed his chin and stared at her.

"And what? With money, she can choose any man she wants."

"Umm, I'd rather an Irish lass like Deidre or Jenny. I don't think our cousin likes me."

"None of those can afford you. They like nice things. No, our cousin is your only hope, but you have to court her, make her think you love her. Americans believe in love. They're dotty with it."

"Tell her I love her instead of her money, eh, Moira?" Ewan looked mischievous.

"I've tried to tell you, business is bad, very bad. With the tourists not coming, the shops that take my goods are cutting back. Even the online orders are off."

"Just convince her to invest in the business."

"She's not stupid and can see how bad things are. No, you have to convince her you love her. Marry her and you get control of her money."

Ewan snorted. "I'm not interested in what comes with the money. You want me to sell meself for thirty pence, eh?"

Moira began to remove the dishes from the table and pile them in the sink. "It's your future that worries me. With your tastes, you need a rich wife. You won't work, so what's left?"

"Your suggestion doesn't please me, but you have a point." Ewan remained silent for a moment. "I like my comfort, so if our meddlesome cousin consents, I'll court the biddy. She poses an interesting challenge, but I always liked those. Sure the woman doesn't exist who can refuse a Clare man."

"You'd best show more respect. She's not one to take kindly to your attitude." With a sigh of disgust, Moira turned to washing the dishes. She hoped Ewan would succeed, if not...

* * * *

Once the *Seabird* docked, the Scandinavians hopped out and took off with long, quick strides for the buildings beyond the dock. Captain Kehoe held Tula's arm to help her to the dock. The warm pressure of his hand almost brought a blush to her face. His glance held hers a long moment.

His broad smile and twinkling blue eyes hinted at something more, but Geneva stood at his elbow ready to disembark. With a half sigh, he turned to the older woman and steadied her. With Jerome behind Geneva in the boat and Tula pulling her arms from the pier, the three managed to get her onto the dock.

Jerome scrambled after her. "I'm for the café. I bet they have some beer. How about you two?"

"Suits me," Geneva said.

"I'll stop by later," Tula replied. "I want to see the island and the seabirds first. Enjoy yourselves."

At the end of the dock, a signpost pointed one way to the café and the other read *To the Birds*. The Kellys turned to the right, and Tula headed left.

The footpath climbed at an easy grade and led upward toward the steep rocky cliffs above. Flocks of sheep grazed on the lower slope, dots of white against the emerald grass. The clouds she had seen from the boat had now thickened and looked somewhat darker. They might bring rain, but she hoped not a heavy storm. Surely, Captain Kehoe would have mentioned that.

They still had the return trip to Dingle. The cabin on the launch was small, even cozy for a few, but cramped for all seven of them. No sense in worrying yet, the clouds would probably pass.

Halfway to the cliff top, seabirds circled above. Besides the ever present seagulls, she saw skuas, gannets, and petrels. Some flew in lazy arcs with others diving toward the sea at dizzying speeds that took her breath away. Then, rapid footfalls on the footpath behind her drew her attention. The path could accommodate two people walking side by side.

So, anyone in a hurry could easily pass her. She turned to see who it was. To her surprise, she recognized Connor Kehoe.

He soon reached her. "You're friends went to the café?"

"Hello," Tula said. "Yes, Jerome likes his comfort, and Geneva wanted to shop. She prefers her scenery at arm's length."

"So I gathered. While I'm glad for clients, I've wondered why they signed up for whale watching and birding. They're not particularly athletic. I suppose they can tell their friends they were here, but not how they spent their time."

"It's Jerome's idea, I think. Geneva said some friend of his recommended seeing the wildlife."

"What about you?" They continued walking side by side along the path, steadily climbing higher.

"Me? I've never been to Ireland," she reminded him and spread her arm wide. "I want to see and do it all."

"It's a fine place. We Irish get homesick if we're long away."

Tula nodded. "Moira did say you went away for a while."

"I did, to attend university, and then a stint in Dublin, but I'm not a city person. I love the west of Ireland."

She couldn't argue with that. "I see, but why tours?"

"Not much else to do. I'm not a fisherman. I worked on the boats once, but it's hard work for little gain. Besides, the fishing's not what it once was. More and more restrictions."

"Seafood is popular."

"Indeed, but with all the foreign factory ships, little is left for the local folks, although a few try sea farming. I hope if people learn to respect the seas and prize the animals, especially the whales and the seabirds, we might preserve our world for a while."

"Even with global warming? You're an idealist." Tula couldn't suppress an amused smile.

"Perhaps, but I find it better to do what I enjoy and do my bit to preserve this world at the same time."

Looking skyward, Tula frowned. The clouds had thickened and grown darker. "Do you think it will rain?"

He studied the clouds for a moment. "We may get a shower, but not a real storm. The cliffs often draw the clouds, and the rain makes the island good grazing for the sheep."

They continued climbing until the path leveled out at the top. Many birds flew overhead and colorful puffins popped out of burrows. Tula blinked at the sight.

"I didn't know the birds nested in the ground."

"Many seabirds do. Some build nests on cliff ledges, but puffins and skuas favor holes in the ground. The puffins use old rabbit warrens. That protects the chicks from other seabirds."

"Can you touch them?"

"Not unless you want to get nipped or attacked. They're wild, not tame. The puffins tolerate tourists walking near their burrows, but not touching them or picking them up. The presence of people keeps the flying predators away."

The puffins, black, feathered bodies, white faces, and rainbow beaks enchanted Tula. To see them in their natural habitat filled her with happiness. It spilled over toward Captain Kehoe. For a man like him to devote his life to preserving and sharing such treasures spoke a lot for his character.

They strolled along until they came to a narrow section of the footpath. Tula went ahead, but stumbled when her right foot landed in a hole. A horrible squawk ensued. A pair of strong arms grabbed her and pulled her aside.

"Careful, that's a skua nest," Captain Kehoe said. "You don't want the adult birds to attack you. They defend their chicks to the death. Right now, you're lucky the parents are out foraging. We'd best move along."

Tula stared down at the dark hole in the ground and shuddered. She had no desire to injure a chick or deal with angry parents. A light mist gathered and rain began to fall.

"There's an overhang ahead if you don't mind sharing it with the wildlife," Captain Kehoe said.

They quickened their pace and soon reached the place where a stone ledge jutted over part of the trail to provide a bit of shelter. Tula ducked under the overhang, followed by the captain. She huddled just past the middle, and he settled next to her. At least the dirt floor remained dry.

"The rain will pass. We Irish call this a soft day. We get a lot of those, so be prepared. They keep Ireland green."

Glad for her wool slacks, sweater, and raincoat, Tula relaxed. However, the dampness made the cold penetrate even those. She marveled that such a mild temperature could chill. Winter in Ohio provided much worse.

Sitting so close to the captain, she appreciated his warmth and he also kept the wind from reaching her. The small space created a welcome, comforting intimacy. The faint scent of his alpine aftershave triggered other pleasant sensations. Immersed in her thoughts, she felt drawn to the captain in a way she hadn't experienced in a long time.

Captain Kehoe rested his head against the back of their shelter. "So how do you find your Ireland and your new kin?"

Shaken from her musings, Tula assumed he knew both Ewan and Moira well and debated what to say. A hint of animosity toward Ewan had surfaced the one time she had seen them together, and she wondered why.

"Ireland I love, while having relatives is new for me. I like Moira. It's nice to have someone who remembered my father. He never came back to Ireland after he went to London, so far as I know, but he painted such beautiful word pictures of it. He never said much about the people of Kilconon though."

The captain looked surprised, but said nothing.

"As for Ewan... I don't like his driving or his attitude. I told Moira I won't ride with him again."

Captain Kehoe laughed. "I canna say I'm surprised. One day he'll wreck that machine, and I hope he survives it. It would destroy Moira if he killed himself. She's mothered him since her mam died."

"Perhaps he'll settle down."

"So Moira hopes, but who would he marry? The local colleens haven't any money, and we don't have any rich widows hereabouts. He'll have to look elsewhere. Moira ought to marry Rory Doyle. He loves her, but she probably thinks he couldn't cope with Ewan. She underestimates him."

"I don't think I've met Mr. Doyle."

"He's the grocer and has a small farm. His mam died last year. Most Irish men marry late. 'Tis hard for two women to share one house, especially if both are Irish."

She laughed, remembering the old saying. "Too many cooks...'"

"Moira speaks of you often," Tula said. She suspected her cousin's interest was in marrying the captain. She held her breath, realizing he might resent her prying.

The captain laughed. "Humph, much as I like and respect Moira, she's a friend, nothing more. Life's too short not to build a relationship on more than that. Even love may not be enough..."

It hadn't been for her and Mario, but she still didn't know how she really felt about him. His suave urbanity, good looks, and success had attracted her, but had she loved him? Sometimes, after so many different relationships, she wondered if she could really love any man. Her pride took a blow when he broke off their relationship, but if he didn't love her, how could she love him? *Basta.*

Conscious of Captain Kehoe, who appeared lost in his own thoughts, she wondered what prompted him to think love wasn't enough. Had he suffered a broken relationship? That led her to wonder what he thought of her, but she wasn't certain she really wanted to know. To her, he was a man and not a callow youth like Ewan. Better yet, he was committed to lofty goals and making positive change possible here. He had much to admire, and coupled with rugged good looks, he offered distinct possibilities.

Ewan had the compelling appearance of her father. That stopped her for a moment. No, he wasn't anything like her father. Charming, yes, but so were most Irish men of a certain age. With him, self-confidence had mushroomed into arrogance.

Staring beyond the ledge, Tula observed the clouds looked less fierce, and the rain had eased. Scrambling to her feet, she moved to the edge of the overhang. "We can finish our walk."

"Indeed, you'll want to get to the café and look around before we leave."

Together, they retraced the path back to the dock area.

"I've enjoyed our walk, Miss Mohr. Thanks for your company. I have to check on our vessel, so you have about thirty minutes for tea and to check out the gift shop. If you see the Lindstroms or the Kellys, would you tell them?" Captain Kehoe tipped his cap and headed toward the mooring.

Murder In Her Mind

* * * *

By the time Connor's guests boarded for the return trip to Dingle, the clouds had dispersed. Tula Mohr sat with Jerome Kelly and the three Lindstroms in the stern. Mrs. Kelly sat in the corner of the cabin. Once underway, she dozed. Connor guessed jet lag had caught up with her.

Half way to Dingle, Connor fixed a pot of tea in the galley and took it to those sitting in the stern. After serving them all, he poured a mug for himself and perched between Tula and Jerome. Like Geneva, Jerome soon dozed.

Connor studied Tula Mohr, pleased by what he saw. Despite the weather, she glowed. Her dark hair formed a nimbus around her face. She hadn't complained about the rain, and appeared to enjoy the trek along the cliff top.

"Did you like the island?"

She gave an emphatic nod. "Yes, especially the puffins. Somehow I've always associated colorful birds with the tropics."

"Ireland has plenty of wildlife, and many seabirds nest in the islands and on the coast. I'm sorry we haven't seen many whales today. Even the small minkes seem to be hiding."

"Do you see a lot of whales?"

"A fair number. The easiest to spot are the orcas, but we don't see a lot of large animals."

"That probably makes it harder to attract whale watchers."

"Ireland provides the big attraction. The Dingle peninsula draws visitors, especially after the American movies and documentaries. Birdwatchers always come for the birds. So it's fairly steady, not huge, but enough. We've had more cruise ships coming, but they stick to major ports and leave the wee islands to the locals."

Tula watched the circling seagulls overhead. "I've been considering starting a B&B. I've yet to see Mohr Cottage, but it might do."

"You've only just arrived. It's a little early for such a major decision. You'd have to have a fair bit to invest. Then you have to get licenses and list with the Tourist Board and all that. It would also mean applying for residency." He paused for a moment, studying her face. "If you decide to do it, let me know. I might be able to help you avoid the shoals."

"I'll do that, and thanks for the offer."

"Well, time for me to steer the boat again." He collected the empty mugs and took them with the teapot into the cabin. The American woman continued to surprise him.

Chapter Nine

Just before docking, Connor went to check on Mrs. Kelly, who had retired to the small cabin. As he descended the steps, she woke and stretched. She looked around the snug cabin as if uncertain where she found herself.

"Afternoon, ma'am," Connor said with a half-smile. "We're about to dock at Dingle town. You might want to join your husband in the stern."

"What? Oh. Yes, thank you." Still a bit befuddled, she stumbled up the steps to the stern.

Connor shook his head and wondered, yet again, why so many tourists looked anything but fit. He'd been glad to see Tula Mohr was a walker and had no trouble climbing the rocky path to the cliff top. This time of day a lot of boats returned to Dingle Bay, so docking took all of his attention as he threaded a course past them.

Nearing the pier, he slowed the forward motion of the boat to approach as close as possible and reversed the engine. Donny stood ready to grab the line and fend the boat from the desired berth. Connor cut the engine and went to help Donny. His passengers gathered their belongings and stood ready to disembark.

Someone had tipped up the blue cushion to clear the seat for easy footing. The Lindstroms had already gone. Miss Mohr and Jerome pushed and shoved to get Mrs. Kelly up and over the side. Connor rushed to help, but before he reached them, they had already managed it.

He took Tula Mohr's hand to assist her, and she smiled at him. He enjoyed her sunny smile; it bathed her whole face in joy. With reluctance, he turned to help Jerome step on the seat and from thence to the dock.

"There you are, Cousin," Ewan called as he approached Miss Mohr

with a wide smile. "Moira's waiting dinner for us. The car's just there."
He pointed to the Viper parked near the dock.

"I told Moira I wouldn't ride with you again, Ewan," she snapped,
clearly annoyed.

"I've come all this way just to take you back," he protested, all
innocence. "A wee ride won't hurt you, Cousin. I promise to drive ever
so slow."

"I'll take a taxi, thank you."

"No need for a taxi, Miss Mohr," Connor interposed. "The boat trip
includes a return to your lodgings."

She flashed him a grateful smile.

"Now, Cousin, sure I'm the best driver in Kerry County," Ewan said
in a wheedling voice.

"The fastest maybe, not the safest." The asperity in her tone amused
Connor, but angered Ewan.

"Have it your way, Cousin." He turned to Connor. "Remember,
she's a customer, nothing more. None of your wiles on my cousin. As
head of the family, I have the final say."

Eyes blazing, the American stepped forward. "No one, I mean no
one, tells me with whom I may ride, talk to, or whatever. Come,
Conner." She reached for his arm. "Let's take the Kellys back to Mrs.
Kennedy's."

"Thanks for the offer," Jerome said, "but Geneva and I are having
dinner here. Hope we see you again." He took Geneva's arm.

"Yes, Tula, you know where we are," Geneva added with a yawn.
"We'll be here a few days more. Thank you, Captain Kehoe, for the
smooth trip." She yawned again and let Jerome lead her away.

Ewan stared with narrowed eyes at Connor, flicked an enigmatic
glance at his cousin, then spun on his heel, and stalked off.

"Donny, can you take the Seabird to her mooring?" Connor said to
his helper.

"You mean it, Captain?" His hopeful look amused Connor.

"Yes, I'll be back later to check on it. Just be sure to lock the cabin."
He tossed the keys to Donny.

Miss Mohr said almost nothing in the van as they drove toward
Kilconon. Connor guessed Ewan had struck a sore nerve. Americans

never liked to be told what to do, at least not the ones he'd met. He hoped this time Ewan had met his match in the willowy American.

When they reached Moira's, to Connor's disappointment, Miss Mohr hopped out before he managed to get out to help her. "Thanks for a great trip and for telling me about the seabirds. I enjoyed this trip more than anything else I've seen."

"You haven't been here long or seen much," Connor replied, smiling. "Kilconon is pretty, but a wee town. You have to see the cities, especially Cork and Dublin. There's also the gardens. Ireland is famous for its gardens. Of course, you haven't yet seen the Cliffs of Moher and the Burren. They're not to be missed. I'd be more than happy to take you to the Cliffs and then on to the Burren." He held his breath waiting for her answer.

She studied his face for a moment and then smiled. "I'd like that. First, Moira and I have to see Mohr Cottage tomorrow. After that, let me know when you plan to take the next group and I'll tag along."

"Indeed, ma'am, I look forward to it." He tipped his cap and watched her enter the cottage. Anticipation at seeing her again buoyed his spirits as he drove home.

Chapter Ten

Fog. A damp, wet veil obscured everything. Cassie MacLeod recognized no landmark, nothing to identify this place. It existed out of time, even out of place… Somewhere else. Light came from nowhere and everywhere. A pale, whitish light, more like moonlight than sunlight, permeated the scene. Cold encased her and she rubbed her arms for warmth.

To the right, a sharp-edged black rock jutted alongside her. Looking down, she saw hard-packed sand. A noise, a sort of murmuring filled the air. Water surged toward her and forced Cassie to step back. A lake or the ocean? Large boulders rose in jumbled heaps and forced her toward the hungry waves.

Ahead, a tall shape moved along the narrow strip of sand. The slim form ahead reminded Cassie of her friend Tula, but she was in Ireland. What was she doing here?

A raucous sound intruded, eerie and filled with grief or warning. The hoarse call of some seabird? She gazed up in a vain attempt to pierce the enveloping murk.

From above, a black shadow swooped towards Tula. As it plunged down, features emerged. A black rapier of a beak, curved sharp talons spread wide, huge wings opening and closing as it flew. Then wings furled, it plummeted at the woman, a missile locked on a target. Death hurled toward her friend.

"TULA," Cassie shouted. "Look out!"

* * * *

"Cassie, Cassie, wake up."

Horrified and confused, she opened her eyes to see Ian, her husband,

70

staring at her.

"What is it? You were thrashing about and shouting Tula's name." He held her close. "A dream?"

Ian's warmth reassured her, but Cassie shuddered as she struggled to let go of the dream images. She lay in her own bed with Ian, not walking on a mist-cloaked seashore.

"Something... something attacked Tula." She stared at him, eyes wide, wanting to disbelieve the vision.

"Was it... was it one of those dreams?" Ian wore a worried look.

Cassie chewed her lower lip, trying to decide. "I'm... not sure. Maybe I'm just upset about Tula because we haven't heard from her."

"Honey, it's only been a couple of days. Did she say she'd call?"

"No, but we always keep in touch."

Cassie scrunched the quilt between her fingers. She knew she worried too much about things. Yet past events wouldn't allow her to dismiss any dream so lightly. Too often, her dreams came as a warning, especially those with threatening animals. That awful crow meant something, but she had no idea what. Maybe Leah had heard from Tula.

"Why don't you call Leah in the morning?" Ian said, echoing her thoughts. "Now, try to sleep." He tucked the blankets around her.

His nearness and warmth helped. Cassie struggled to relax, but the image of the malevolent bird kept her awake. Sometime, much later, she slept.

* * * *

In the morning, Cassie called Leah and arranged to meet her for lunch at Tula's Tearoom. Determined to find some answers, she arrived fifteen minutes early at the rendezvous.

Under Kinesha's management, the restaurant looked the same as always with its square tables covered with cheerful yellow or green tablecloths. The usual small vases of white daisies graced the tables. Several couples sat near the window, testifying that the place functioned in Tula's absence.

Kinesha, Tula's capable assistant manager, smiled at Cassie as she entered. "Good to see you, Cassie. Leah's at your usual table in back."

"Thanks." Cassie hurried to join her friend and slid onto a chair adjacent to Leah. The spicy aroma from a pot of Tula's Special Blend scented the air.

"Hi, Leah. Thanks for coming." Cassie sniffed the fragrant tea bouquet. "Umm, I need a cup of that."

Leah poured steaming tea into a yellow mug and pushed it toward Cassie. "Good for what ails your spirit, Tula always says."

After another whiff of the rich aroma, Cassie sipped the spicy brew. One taste soothed her tattered spirits. She released a long sigh. "That always helps."

"Okay, what's the panic?" Leah gazed at her, a frown on her face.

At that moment, Kinesha approached them. "Would you like Tula's Moroccan Salads? I also have some fresh, black currant scones, and there's still a bit of clotted cream."

"Sounds fabulous, Kinesha." Leah looked to Cassie. "Okay with you?"

Cassie smiled at Kinesha. "Yes, especially those scones. Kinesha, have you heard from Tula?"

"No, but I'm sure she'll be nagging me in a day or two. She worries I can't manage without her." Kinesha gave them a broad smile. "I'll be right back with your lunch." She hurried through the beaded curtain to the kitchen.

"Okay, Cassie, give," Leah said. "What's bugging you?"

"I had a dream last night." Cassie stared down at the brown liquid in her cup and clasped it with both hands. Warmth seeped from the tea, through the cup, and into her encircling fingers.

"Ah, one of those … dreams?" Leah stared at her with a worried face.

"I'm… I'm not sure. The haze in the dream made it hard to see anything. I glimpsed a shape. A woman, I think. She was walking on a beach. To me, she looked about Tula's height, but she blended into the darkness and the fog. Then, out of nowhere, this huge black bird swooped down." Cassie shuddered. "It had a long, razor-sharp beak and wicked claws."

Leah blinked and stared at her. "Claws? Birds don't have claws."

Cassie shrugged. "Talons, whatever. They looked dangerous. That bird meant to injure or even kill the woman."

Frowning, Leah leaned forward and took Cassie's hand in hers. "You didn't watch Hitchcock's *The Birds*, did you?"

"No way, you know I don't like horror movies, even Hitchcock's. Last time Tula thought it was the *Attack of the Killer Rabbits*. That rabbit represented Brad Harrison, remember?"

"Yeah, I remember. I also remember Arboc, the cobra, from your dream about Ted." Leah paused for moment, thinking. "Hmm, just trying to make sure something else didn't trigger your dream. All right, what happened next?"

Before Cassie could say more, Kinesha returned with a tray and placed salads in front of each of them. She added a plate of warm scones and a small dish of clotted cream in the middle of the table.

"Enjoy," she said and hurried toward the front of the tearoom to greet a couple just entering.

Leah nibbled her lip. "Okay, tell me the rest."

"I … I shouted to warn the woman. Guess my shouting woke Ian, because the next I knew he was shaking me. Have you heard from Tula?"

"No, not yet." Leah reached for a scone. After covering it with a bit of the cream, she took a bite and chewed. "Ahh. Tula ought to patent these or whatever to protect her recipe. She's my kind of chef—exotic, tasty, and always a delight."

"I know," Cassie agreed. "But what about Tula?"

Sighing, Leah set the remainder of the scone down. "Realistically, she's only been gone a few days."

"Yes, Ian said that, but anything can happen in a few days. I'm scared, Leah. That bird terrified me." Cassie shuddered.

"If Tula were here, she'd ask you what the bird represented." Leah began to eat her salad.

Cassie gave her a blank look. "How would I know? Danger? An enemy? Tula's the expert, not me. It took all three of us to work out the identity of the cobra, remember?"

Leah sighed. "I wish Tula were here. Gypsy lore, I understand, but I don't know a lot about Irish myths. A black bird?"

Nodding, Cassie continued. "Yeah, inky black, almost as if cut from night itself. Sort of like Poe's raven, but large. More like a condor."

"'Quoth the Raven, 'Nevermore.'' If I remember right, the raven, or was it a crow, is an omen of death."

"That's kinda what I thought." Shivering, Cassie rubbed her arms. "It's the reason I'm scared for Tula and why we have to warn her."

"Well, we're here and she's there somewhere. She didn't give us a telephone number to call because she didn't know where she'd be staying. The only thing I can think of is for both of us to email her." Leah sighed, clearly frustrated. "Sometimes Tula can be too self-assured and cavalier. About all I can do is to try reading the Tarot cards and see if they have anything to tell us."

Cassie nodded. "Please. Once dreams like this start, they keep returning. I couldn't bear it if anything happened to Tula and we hadn't tried to warn her. I guess I could do a search on that place she went. Kilconon, wasn't it?"

"Yeah, do it, and don't forget to send an email to her too. Anyway, call me and let me know what you learn and I'll do the same. You might also look up crow or birds in Irish myths."

"Okay, I will." Cassie relaxed, glad to have something constructive to do.

"Now, let's eat. This food is too good to not enjoy it." Leah took another mouthful of the Moroccan Salad.

Chapter Eleven

Connor's mobile rang as he drove away from Moira's cottage.

"Connor? Donny here. Someone's been mucking about your boat. I'd swear it was that Ewan. I saw him in the stern. No idea what he was doing, but mischief I'm sure."

"Thanks, Donny, I'm on my way." Connor disconnected and hit the petrol pedal. Tula would accuse him of doing an Ewan as the van leapt forward.

Luckily, the road was empty of cars, sheep, and cows. He made it to the dock in fifteen minutes.

Donny waited for him by the dinghy. "You want I should come too?"

"No, you'd best wait here and keep your eye on things. I'll be back as soon as I make certain nothing is wrong."

Connor pushed off and rowed toward the *Seabird*. Whatever Ewan had done would only bring trouble. When he reached his boat, he tied up the dinghy and climbed aboard. He first checked the cabin door, but the lock showed no tampering. A quick check of the hatches revealed nothing.

He gazed around the stern looking for anything out of place. Opening the lockers beneath the seats revealed only the usual gear. He moved lines aside, a spare anchor, and life jackets, but still nothing.

Puzzled, he stood up and tried to think. He had no idea what mischief Ewan intended, but suspected it would cause him major trouble. He looked down at the pedestal. Situated in the middle of the stern area, it had no lock. He opened the top and peered inside. The plastic canisters with powdered milk and sugar packets sat snug in their places. He stared down at them trying to outguess Ewan. Unable to think of anything, he

75

lifted the canisters and then swore at what he saw. Beneath the sugar lay two wee plastic envelopes. They looked like…

"May the Hounds of Hell take you, Ewan Clare." He removed the pouches, shoved them in a pocket, and closed the pedestal.

Furious, Connor hurried to the dinghy and lowered himself over the side. Best to dump these things before the Garda came nosing around. If they ever found contraband, he'd end in gaol and they'd confiscate the *Seabird*. When he got his hands on bloody Ewan Clare, he'd throttle him, Moira's brother or no.

Connor raised the oars and rowed away from his boat toward the dock. Midway, he stopped and pulled the plastic pouches from his jacket. He bent over the side as if checking the boat and emptied, first one packet, and then the other into the bay. The white powder floated away in lazy arcs carried by the waves. He released the empty packets and watched them float for a moment. He pushed on them with the oar until they sank. Satisfied, he headed for the dock.

There, Donny grabbed the painter and hauled the boat close. Connor shipped the oars, handed them to Donny, and scrambled onto the dock.

"You find anything, Captain?"

"Yeah, Ewan's git. If he comes around again, call me, no matter what the time." Connor slipped Donny a couple of euros.

Debating what to do about Ewan, Connor remained reluctant to accuse him or tell the Garda about the idiot. Still, he needed to protect the *Seabird* and himself. As he considered the options, he saw Sean Jamison, a member of the local Garda ahead. Just the man.

Nodding at the officer, Connor approached him. "Evening, Sean. How's business?"

"Mostly quiet, Connor. Once the pubs close, it'll get rowdy. If not the locals, there are a few tourists who have a pint too many than is wise."

"Too true. I'm here because my watchman called to tell me he thought someone had been messing around the *Seabird*. Luckily, when I checked her, I didn't find any problem, but I'd appreciate it if you and your fellow officers would keep an eye on her for a while."

Sean laughed. "We watch all the boats. We've an alert out just now about some foreign cartel trying to smuggle drugs. It's the Spanish this time." Sean sighed and shook his head. "Some scum never learn. The Coasties have feelers out and check everything afloat, especially the yachts and the fishing boats. Surprised they've missed you."

"I didn't know, but I want nothing to do with drugs or smuggling. It would destroy my business. You can rest easy. If I hear anything, I'll pass it on."

"With the 'eyes in the sky,' the Coasties know where every freighter, cruise ship, yacht, fishing boat, and even your *Seabird* are. There's no hiding anymore." Sean gave Connor a knowing wink and then turned serious. "You're from Kilconon, aren't you? There's talk about Ewan Clare and his speedboat."

"Oh? I'm sorry to hear that. I hope for his sister's sake, it isn't true." Now it was his turn to shake his head.

"He's not a friend of yours, is he?" Sean studied Connor under the nearby wharf light.

"He lives in Kilconon, I know him and his sister, Moira. Can't say I ever liked Ewan much. He's a troublemaker, always has been."

"Too true. He drives too fast. Billy's determined to catch him, but it'll take a sturdy roadblock to stop that machine of his."

"Billy has my best wishes on that," Connor said. "He tailgated my van the other day. I had passengers, so I couldn't deal with him then. Next time he won't get off like that."

"Best call Billy and let him handle it. Do you want to file complaint?"

"I'll give it thought. Well, it's getting late and I best get home. I have to be up early tomorrow to take some tourists to see the sights. As I said earlier, I'd appreciate a watch on the *Seabird*."

"I'll tell the others. Glad you told me; we want no trouble in Dingle. Evening, Connor."

"Evening, Sean." Connor strolled off, his hands in his pockets. Ewan had best take care.

* * * *

After returning to Kilconon, Connor sat with Rory Doyle near the fireplace in the Kilconon Arms and sipped pints of ale.

"So how goes it?" Rory studied Connor's flushed face.

Connor shrugged. "Mixed. Business is down some, but I have bookings for the season. Hope the cargo business improves this winter, else I'm for selling my boat." He stared at the glowing peat in the fireplace.

"The mess in Dublin and elsewhere affects us all. I'm fortunate folks still need to eat, but they buy only what they must. If not for my garden supplying fresh veggies, I'd be in sad shape. I miss Mam. She did a lot." Rory frowned, unlike his usual easy-going way.

Nodding in agreement, Connor grinned. "You need a wife."

"Aye, but Moira isn't interested." He heaved a heartfelt sigh.

"There's Jenny." Connor nodded toward the plump barmaid.

"Ah no, she wants to go to Dublin or Cork. She's no interest in a farm and a small town grocer." Rory lifted his pint. "Too few prospects here."

"Well, there's Moira's cousin." Curious how Rory saw Tula Mohr, Connor watched his friend for a reaction.

"She's a beaut, but I can't see her on a farm. Too elegant for that. Besides, I thought Ewan had plans for her."

Connor snorted. "So he told me, but she's a mind of her own. No man will drive her unless she wants to go that way. My guess is, she thinks him a reckless layabout." He leaned back and sipped his pint.

From his grin, Rory shared the same view of Ewan. "Well, you might consider her yourself."

"I might, but I doubt she'd consider me. Besides, I'm still trying to get my business going. Kilconon is likely to prove too quiet for her." Connor stared at the fire in silence, mulling over what the future might hold and how soon Tula Mohr would be leaving. He hoped she'd stay awhile.

He'd never met anyone quite like the striking American. She'd impressed him with her spunk, exotic beauty, and intelligence. Few women did that anymore. Once burned, a man grew cautious. At his age, it wouldn't do to make mistakes. Besides, at present she was a customer, not a friend.

Rory's glass clinked as he set it down. "Moira's having a hard time of it—too few tourists coming and the locals can't afford what she asks. As for her herbs and all the rest, even that trade is down."

"Too true. The whole country is suffering."

"For her, it's Ewan." Rory looked troubled.

"She's spoiled him. He should be working," Connor groused. "Maybe that would keep him out of trouble."

"Aye, but at what and where?" Sighing, Rory shook his head. "Too few jobs and too many want them."

Connor sipped his pint, debating whether to tell Rory about Ewan's nastiness aboard the Seabird. "He tried to get me to carry some illicit cargo for him. Of course, I said no. Too risky. I'd never do that. Tonight, he left a wee present on the *Seabird*."

"What?" Rory stared at him in disbelief.

"Contraband, most likely drugs. Donny alerted me, and I got rid of the stuff. Sean stopped me for a chat."

Rory looked shocked at the news. "Not serious I hope."

"No, not for me. Sean hinted they suspect Ewan of smuggling, but haven't the evidence yet. Everyone knows he's desperate for money."

Frowning, Rory picked up his glass. "Sorry I am to hear that. That car of his must cost dear. I fear for Moira if they catch him."

"He thinks he's a right to the best. When I see him, he's for a hiding." Connor tightened his hand on the glass and squeezed, wishing he had Ewan by the throat. "Moira should get rid of the car. One of these days he'll wreck it and kill himself, and who knows who else."

"Indeed, I've told her so. Ewan needs a strong hand." A sad look crossed Rory's face, and he shook his head.

"She's left it too late for that," Connor muttered.

"Connor, she needs help from us."

"The woman won't listen any more than Ewan himself. The Clares are above all that." He didn't bother to hide the bitterness in his voice. "Anyway, I'm the wrong man. I like Moira, but I don't love her, and Ewan would cause no end of troubles, especially if anyone came down hard on the slacker."

"Aye, but she's a good woman," Rory protested.

"That she is and you"—Connor grinned at Rory—"fancy her."

"Too right. Ever since we were children I've tried to protect her, but she'll have none of me. I thought, with my mam gone, she might change." He said nothing more for a bit and then roused himself. "Moira admires you, Connor. I want her to be happy."

"So do I, Rory, but it wouldn't work. I tried with one woman, remember? Unless you both love, it's no go."

"We're in the same stew pot." Rory lifted his glass and drained the last of it. "I'd best be off. The cats get restless unless I feed them."

"Too bad women aren't as easy to please." Connor drank the remains of his pint and followed Rory out the door.

Chapter Twelve

The next day after breakfast, Tula and Moira set out at a brisk pace along the road north of the village. After a half hour walk, they came to a small stone building, a story-and-a-half cottage with a real estate sign in front. The gray walls appeared solid enough, and the windows remained unbroken.

"This is Mohr Cottage, Tula," Moira said. "It's seen better days."

Tula approached the green front door, which appeared functional, despite the faded and peeling paint. She peered in one of the dusty windows. Inside, a pile of thatch filled one corner, and the sky showed through a large hole in the roof.

"We can ask Rory Doyle for the key if you want to see inside, but you'd best be careful. It's likely the rest of the roof could fall."

Walking around the house, Tula stopped to glance in other windows as she circled the cottage. The ground floor housed the living room with a fireplace, another small room—most likely for dinning—a kitchen, and a mudroom-cum-utility. Stairs led to an upper story. She hoped the place had two bedrooms and a bath up there, but whatever, she could add an annex if needed. The mudroom would house the laundry, shelves for storage, and maybe a half bath. The space would be tight, but should work.

Back at the front, she stopped and faced Moira. "We need to ask for the key. When we come back, I'd like to see upstairs."

Moira frowned and shook her head. "You'd have to spend too much to make it livable. Then, what would you do with it? It might be all right for a summer visit, but Kilconon's off the main road. Why would anyone come here?" She looked unhappy and puzzled.

"Just look around you." Tula waved toward the village with its one church and the Kilconon Arms, both sturdy stone and timber buildings, and the sloping hills rising beyond the village. "This place is so picturesque. Besides that, tourists like to discover out-of-the-way places. If you'll share some of your recipes, I could provide a combination of Irish, American, and Somali food. I guarantee the gourmets and gourmands would find Mohr Cottage."

"Tula, what do you mean?" Moira stared at her as if doubting her sanity.

"If I decide to stay, I'll need some form of income. I was thinking about a B&B."

"What?" Moira looked shocked. "No, it's a … a … hopeless idea. It wouldn't work."

"Yes, it would. People always say that about something new and untried." Tula paused a moment. "Besides, with the Europeans coming, such trade can only grow."

Pinching her lips together, Moira looked decidedly unhappy. "Perhaps, but it would take so much money. Better to spend it on other things."

Laughter assailed Tula at her cousin's attitude. "I'm an orphan. I spend my money as I like, and could probably get some business loans from the right places."

"Loans?" A bitter laugh testified to Moira's scorn. "Maybe a year ago, but now? I doubt it. You'd best save your money. If you want to invest, why not become a partner in my business? I could use the capital. The bank wants to call in my letter of credit."

"I'm sorry to hear that, Moira." She paused a moment and studied her cousin's face. "Why not sell that car of Ewan's and make him get a job?"

"The car isn't his; he only leases it. As for jobs, doing what? For a while, the internet provided opportunities, but it's not so good of late," Moira acknowledged. "As for Ewan, he went to the university. He deserves better than working as a laborer or a fisherman."

"Then he must have some skills. What was his major?"

"University degrees are plentiful," Moira snapped. "It means nothing. Graduates have to go overseas for jobs."

"It might help."

"No, Tula. He'll not leave Kilconon; Maeve is buried here. This is his home."

Having met Ewan, laziness seemed more likely to Tula. He had no incentive to do anything, so long as Moira kept him. Her respect for both her cousins was in rapid decline.

"What about teaching? Surely there's a demand for teachers?"

"With twenty candidates for each opening, he has nary a chance. Besides, they're all elsewhere. At least here, he knows people and they know him."

Tula shook her head, remembering Ewan flirting with every young woman he saw. She couldn't imagine someone like Connor employing a wastrel like Ewan.

"I'm sorry, Moira, but he should help you, not drag you down. Surely, the farms, shops, or the boats could use a good pair of hands. Pubs are popular and they employ people."

"We're Clares," Moira insisted. "He's got too much ambition for that."

"Then he'd better find a rich widow or an heiress," Tula snapped and then wished she hadn't. Moira must already have that in mind with her as the "wealthy" bride.

"Not in Kilconon, Cousin," Moira responded.

"Anyway, he's your problem, Moira. He may be a distant cousin of mine, but he's not my responsibility." She walked toward the road, unwilling to encourage more thoughts of her money in Moira's mind.

"Tula, if you want to see inside, you'd best stop by the store and ask Rory for the key," Moira called after her.

Disillusioned by Moira's coddling of Ewan, Tula fumed as she walked down the road in the direction of Kilconon. She liked helping people, but refused to waste her time on those who expected others to solve their problems. In truth, she had only just met Moira and Ewan, and at best, they were distant cousins.

While Tula liked Moira, she lacked sufficient knowledge of what her cousin needed to do or to advise her on her business. She knew little more than what Moira told her. As for Ewan, actions spoke far louder than words. Coddling him was not the answer. As for that car of his... Tula ground her teeth. Little boys didn't need expensive toys.

* * * *

Beyond the village, Tula soon found the steep path to the beach Moira had mentioned earlier, and started down it to the sand and rocks below. The narrow path zigzagged and edged around rocky outcrops. At times, it almost vanished, but Tula persisted and soon reached the shore.

Once there, restless waves washed over rugged, black rock outcroppings jutting out from the shore. The waves clashing against the rocks created a salt haze that made seeing any distance difficult.

Taking a deep breath of the sea air, Tula released a pleased sigh as she strolled along the base of the cliff. The invigorating salt tang of the sea refreshed her spirits. The brilliant blue sky above, the roiling water with white foam eating at the land, and the wet rocks, black and glistening, cast a hypnotic spell over her. Only this place and this moment existed.

Change had come to her, pushed by circumstances and her friends. In their view, she had a broken heart, which distance and time would heal. She didn't see it as that. Yes, she hadn't expected Mario's decision to break off things, but if she was honest, they had fallen into friendship, not love. Something was missing from her life, but she wasn't sure it was a man.

In Columbus and elsewhere, she had friends, good friends, and many acquaintances, and now she'd found two new cousins. She didn't face loneliness, and she enjoyed solitude. As she considered her life now, what it lacked was challenge. Mohr House could provide that.

She had always loved challenges and faced them head-on. After her parents died, she used part of her inheritance to open Tula's Tearoom in Columbus. The venture had thrived. It was no longer a challenge.

Above, noisy seagulls drew Tula from her thoughts. Here was the real Ireland with all its beauty and magic. In the distance, a small stream trickled down the cliff face and formed a pool at the base of the tall cliffs. From there, it flowed in a slow, silver thread to the ocean.

As she approached closer to the stream, a hump on a large rock resolved into a huddled form—a kneeling woman with a pile of something beside her. Clothes? The woman held up a tunic, or perhaps a shirt, shook it out, and then doused it in the water. Up and down, up and down, in rhythm with the waves. After a bit, she hit the garment against the rock face and then submerged it again. To Tula, the woman looked as if she was washing the garment.

Apparently satisfied with her work, the woman wrung water from the garment and spread it over a nearby rock. Tula stared, unable to believe anyone did laundry in such a labor intensive way or in cold, possibly salty, water. She had heard there were parts of Dingle that followed the old ways, but this seemed to be extreme.

Perhaps the stream wasn't salty, but still, why carry laundry to the beach? Tula hadn't noticed any dwellings while she descended the path, nor seen any along the beach. Provided the woman spoke English, she could tell Tula about the beach and what she doing.

The circling seagulls swooped down looking for scraps, or maybe crabs or sand worms. A squabble broke out between two large birds until one grabbed whatever the prize was from the other and flew off toward the cliff top. As Tula followed the bird's flight, she glimpsed a dark object at the cliff edge.

In the next instant, everything changed.

The dark object hurtled from the cliff edge in a downward arc. It had to be a dislodged boulder. Time slowed. If she didn't move, the huge rock would hit her. Horrified, she scrambled back and hugged the side of the cliff. Eyes wide, she grasped her sun pendant and held her breath.

Chapter Thirteen

The huge rock's trajectory ruffled Tula's hair and almost grazed her as it plowed into the sand inches from her feet. Horrified, she stared from it to the top of the cliff, but saw no one there or any reason why it should have fallen.

Looking back to the stream, Tula no longer saw the woman or her laundry. No one strolled along the shingle in either direction. In the distance offshore, a few boats bobbed, and a large ship sailed north, far out to sea.

The gray-black boulder lay half buried in the soft sand in front of her. If it had hit her…

Moira didn't know where she had gone. No one knew, except possibly that woman by the stream, but there was no way to tell if she had witnessed the abrupt descent of the boulder.

Her peaceful mood destroyed, Tula hurried on shaky legs back to the path up the cliff. At the top, she walked to a spot above where the boulder had fallen. She examined the ground, but found little beyond a few smaller rocks. Perhaps time and wind had loosened its hold, but why had it fallen just when she passed that point?

The stony ground showed no evidence of footprints. Puzzled, she started back toward Kilconon in a confused jumble of thoughts and speculations. She had made no enemies in Ireland. So far, she had met only a few people. She might have upset Ewan, but he had no reason to want her dead. They were cousins, and families mattered in Ireland.

As she passed the grocery store, a broad shouldered, red-haired man emerged and smiled at her. "You must be Moira's cousin, Tula Mohr." Tula blinked and nodded. "I'm Rory Doyle, a friend of Moira's. Been exploring?"

Still shaken, Tula stumbled over what to say. "I … I went walking on the shingle."

"Nice place that, but you have to watch out for falling rocks. They hit that beach all the time. Didn't Moira tell you?"

Shaking her head, Tula rubbed her arms, cold to the core.

Worry filled Rory's face as he gave her a searching look. "You look a bit down. I'm just stepping over to the pub for a cuppa. Come along."

"What?" Tula clutched her pendant and warmth flowed along her arm. "Umm, tea sounds great. Where?" She looked around and then remembered Kilconon had no teashop.

"The pub over there serves tea. Let me treat you. Any cousin of Moira is a friend." He reached for her arm.

His comment about cousins made her smile, and she assumed he had heard her whole tale from Father Donnelly or Moira herself. Gossip was the staff of life in small villages—that and a pint.

Inside the cozy pub, Tula slid onto the bench nearest fireplace and held her hands toward the warm glow of the peat fire. Rory went to the bar and ordered tea. The welcome heat began to thaw her icy hands.

Observing Rory walking toward her, she was reminded of a large brown bear. His unruly red hair and his wide smile implied strength tempered by good humor. He made her feel safe.

Taking a short, sturdy stool opposite from her, he sat, facing her. "Jenny will bring the tea in a tick." He studied her face for a long moment before speaking. "Maybe you'd like something stronger?"

"No, tea suits me. It's just … just a large boulder almost hit me. It was so unexpected."

Now Rory stared at her with concern in his warm brown eyes. "Most locals know about the boulders. Someone should have told you."

"Moira was busy and maybe assumed I had heard about the rocks. Any beach walker below a cliff knows to watch for falling rocks. Besides, she didn't even know I was going there. The trouble was, I was deep in thought after Moira and I disagreed about Mohr House … and Ewan."

Jenny set the teapot on the table with two cups and added a plate of currant scones with butter. "If you need anything, let me know." She hurried away to the bar.

Tula added milk and a bit of sugar to her cup and poured some tea. A sip of the hot liquid soothed her frazzled nerves. Relaxing, warmth and confidence return. "That's probably why I didn't meet anyone on the beach."

"We lack tourists just now, and the folks about here have too much to do to walk in the middle of the day." Rory grinned at her.

"I'm enjoying Kilconon and everything about it. My father was born here." Tula paused for a moment to sip her tea. "I saw only one woman, an oldish one, washing clothes on the beach."

Rory stared at her, eyes wide. "Washing you say?" He rubbed his chin, looking thoughtful. "I never heard of that. In the old days, maybe, but not now. Women like their comforts too much. If they don't have a washing machine, they go to the launderette. Where did you see the woman?"

"Where the little stream cuts down to the ocean. She was dressed in black and was kneeling on a large rock to wash something."

Frowning, he appeared puzzled at first. "You're quite sure, about the woman, I mean?"

Tula nodded. "I saw her, but after the boulder fell, she had disappeared. I don't know where she went."

Rory studied her face, his own serious. "Ms. Mohr, do you know much about Irish folklore?"

"A bit, but not a lot. Why?"

"Did you ever hear of the 'Washer Woman'?"

Tula thought for a moment. She had never heard anything about washerwomen. "No, I haven't."

"Legend has it that an Irish hero, Cú Chulainn, passed by a stream and saw a woman washing clothes. She had his shirt. Legend says when you see the 'Washer Woman' someone will die."

Fingers of ice tingled across her neck. Tula suppressed a shiver and clutched her warm cup. "Has anyone in Kilconon ever mentioned a washer woman to you?"

Rory said nothing for several minutes. "Can't say I've ever heard of that, but in Ireland no one should discount old tales. Strange things happen here. You know Moira has the second sight?"

"She's never mentioned it." Tula sat a moment, pondering what visions Moira might have had. "I have a close friend who does too."

"Indeed, Moira knew when her mam was dying. She struggled to stop Death, but we all die sometime." Rory paused for several moments. "Perhaps the washer woman came as a warning."

Startled, Tula stared at him. "For me?"

"Not necessarily, but maybe for someone close to you. You're young. Unless you ride with Ewan in that fast car of his, I can't see you dying young." Rory grinned at her, his eyes atwinkle. "Connor mentioned you accompanied the Kellys on the *Seabird*. Tell me, how do like him?"

"Connor?" Rory's abrupt change of topic surprised her. "I like him fine. He's an excellent sailor, a gentleman, and takes good care of his clients. He's hoping to preserve the seabirds."

"Indeed, he wants to make his business succeed, but like Moira, faces hard times just now. I worry about him. He has no kin left and spends all his time on that boat of his, seeking new clients, or looking for cargo runs."

Rory sighed and picked up the teapot. Finding it empty, he signaled to Jenny.

Tula laughed, amused that Connor was so much like her. "He sounds like two other people I know, Moira and me."

"You too? Here I thought you a lady at leisure."

She shook her head. "Don't I wish. No, actually, I don't. It's only right now because I've taken a vacation for the first time in ten years. I came to Ireland to see if any relatives remained."

Rory nodded. "I've heard about your father. What think you of Kilconon? It's wee and quiet, but still a beautiful, unspoiled part of Ireland."

"That's why I'm thinking of buying Mohr Cottage, and perhaps renting it out."

"A worthy project, provided trade recovers. Still, no matter what, Americans will want to come to Ireland. We sent so many folks to America that now their children want to see the old place. An Irishman never forgets his roots."

Jenny approached with a steaming pot. "Taking the morning off, are you, Rory?"

"Well now, I thought I'd get to know our new resident, Miss Tula Mohr."

"Moira's cousin, yes, I know. Well, enjoy. Let me know if you want more scones. Cook baked this morning." Jenny hurried off to answer a bell from the kitchen.

"We'd best sample the scones or the cook might throw them at us." He picked up one, swathed it in butter, and took a generous bite. "Umm, Jenny's right. These are real Irish scones."

Grinning, Tula followed suit and savored the biscuits. The currants and maybe a bit of cinnamon proved irresistible. Finished, she buttered another. "No good for a diet."

"Ah, you've no need to worry. Now, Jenny, maybe, but not you."

They finished the scones and the tea. Tula leaned against the bench back, sated.

He pushed back his chair and stood looking down at her. "Well, even if it's a slow day, I must return to the shop. Thank you for sharing tea with me. You've color in you cheeks again. How do you feel?"

"I'm fine. Guess I have a little too much imagination."

"Ah, just proves you're Irish. I could walk with you to Moira's."

"That's kind, but not necessary. Nerves and the unexpected upset me, but the tea and scones brought me back. Thank you for prescribing them. I've enjoyed meeting and talking with you, Mr. Doyle." Tula rose as well. "Moira said you have the key to Mohr House."

"Yes, the estate agent left it with me. Can't say anyone's asked for it. The walls may be sound, but the roof would have to be replaced. Maybe a new beam or two as well. The thatch is no good and replacing it would be costly. Besides, the present owner bought it when prices were higher, and he wants his money back."

"Moira said as much."

He appeared to be considering the situation. "Few tourists come to Kilconon, so there's not a need for rentals."

She smiled at his assessment, which agreed with Moira's. "I still want to see the inside."

"I'll give you the key any time you want. If you really mean to settle, you could learn a lot about the area and meet the folks of Kilconon at the church jumble sale. Ask Moira to bring you. Lots of odds and ends there. It's to raise money for Father Donnelly's Poor Box. He's finding more needy folks these days."

"That sounds interesting. When is it?"

"Tomorrow. They also serve a lonely supper and cream teas."

"You've made it irresistible." Tula smiled at him. "I should let Moira know I'm all right."

"Do, please. She's a worrier, that one. I hope to see you tomorrow then." Rory held the door for her and then walked toward his store.

Tula watched for a moment before turning toward Moira's cottage. According to Rory, rocks fell to the beach all the time. She decided not to make much of the event. She had no desire to worry Moira. Ewan did that more than enough.

Chapter Fourteen

By the time Tula reached Moira's Cottage, she dismissed the boulder's fall as an accident. She knew too few people to have made any enemies, and had met only a few local Irish. No one had any reason to cause her harm.

When she arrived at the cottage, Moira stared at her for a moment, her eyes wide with surprise. She shook her head and smiled at Tula. "How was the walk?"

"Fine, I had no trouble finding the path to the beach, but it's tricky in places. The place is beautiful. The sky, the sea, and all that water, so much openness. On land, unless the country is like the American plains or the Russian steppes, you only see a small bit at a time. The land here is much more on a human scale."

"I'd not thought of it like that, but that's so. I'll have lunch ready soon."

"I met Rory Doyle when I came through the village. He said something about a church jumble sale and dinner."

"Father Donnelly and the church guild sponsor it every year. I fear this year's sale may be sparse, yet the need for money has grown."

"Do you go?"

"Always. Everyone in Kilconon attends, and even some tourists come. Father Donnelly berates any backsliders. Those too poor to pay for dinner eat anyway. I thought we'd have supper there. Everyone brings a dish to share and the Kilconon Arms contributes a large leg of gammon, and the cook makes scones enough for Dingle." They both laughed.

"Maybe after lunch we could ask Rory for the key to Mohr Cottage. I'd like to see inside."

"I'll have to check online for orders, and then we can go." Moira put on a teakettle to boil.

"I've been meaning to ask you if I could get on to the internet to check my email."

"We can try. Sometimes the connection causes problems."

After a lunch of cheese, pickles, chutney, and dark bread, Moira showed Tula the computer she used for her orders. Tula logged on to the internet with no trouble, but the slow response time annoyed her.

She had told her friends and associates she would be traveling, and to send only urgent messages. After a few minutes and with Moira's help, she retrieved her email. Kinesha, Cassie, and Leah had all sent messages. She started with Kinesha's, relieved to know the Tearoom fared well and no crises had arisen.

```
Enjoy yourself and stop worrying. Kinesha
```

Tula smiled. She opened Cassie's message next.

```
    Please be extra careful. I dreamed again,
one of those. Someone wants to kill you. Watch
out for huge ravens. Love, Cassie.
```

A shiver shook Tula, and she stared open-mouthed at the message. Had the boulder not been an accident? Raven? What raven? She had only seen two seagulls squabbling, and that had saved her from harm.

Symbols. Cassie always dreamed in symbols, and deciphering them took time and ingenuity. What could the raven mean? Poe wrote of a raven, and they often figured in horror stories, but not in real life. Irish myths mentioned crows and ravens. If she remembered correctly, the Irish called the goddess of war the Crow Goddess.

Cassie's warning disturbed her. She shouldn't dismiss it out of hand, but what to make of it?

```
    I've seen no ravens. Have you watched
Hitchcock's 'The Birds' lately? Let me
know if you dream again. How's Ian? Will
try to keep in touch. Take care.
```

Love, Tula

Puzzling over ravens, Tula opened Leah's message.

> Tula, the cards show mixed signs, but warn of trouble. Be careful and don't trust anyone. On a positive note, the Lovers also appeared, so who's the new beau?
> Love, Leah.

Well, at least Leah said mixed signs. As for the Lovers, Ewan had tried, but she couldn't imagine the cards meant him. Such a puppy held no attraction for her. The only other single men she'd met were Rory and Connor. While sympathetic, Rory didn't stir her senses. Connor could, but he hadn't made any overt moves on her. Besides, she hadn't come to Ireland looking for a man, but for her roots and any relatives.

> Leah, no man I know of. I've found two cousins, Moira and Ewan Clare. Moira knits sweaters and sells them online. She knew my grandmother. I'm staying with the Clares.
> Have seen the puffins. Love those little birds. I'm fine, so don't worry about me. Try to help Cassie. Her dreams weigh her down. Take care.
> Love, Tula.

She deleted the rest of the junk mail and signed off.

Tula joined Moira in the living room. "Thanks for letting me use the internet. Not much there, but I told my friends about you and Ewan. I'm sure they're surprised. Everyone thinks I'm an orphan."

"No more; we're a family now. We can get the key to Mohr Cottage from Rory and peek inside, but you best take care. That roof might come down. We've just found each other, and I expect us to share the rest of our lives."

Moira's words touched Tula and sent a welcome warmth through her. "Me too." She hugged Moira, glad to have family.

Twenty minutes later, after retrieving the key from Rory, Tula opened the front door of Mohr Cottage and, with a bit of pushing and tugging, got the door open. Thatch had fallen to the floor in several places. The living room, like Moira's, occupied a large portion of the main floor. A small dining room or study opened at one side. It would do nicely as a breakfast room. A kitchen, a bit larger than Moira's, made up the remainder. A mudroom/pantry adjoined the kitchen and provided access to the back garden.

The kitchen had wooden counters, a porcelain sink, but no stove or fridge. She assumed anything of value had been removed or sold when the Mohrs died out.

She worked her way to the stairs and checked each step as she climbed. At least they hadn't deteriorated. At the top, she faced three doors, one on each side and one at the end. A look through the closest door revealed a square room with a window. The other door concealed the same. The last door contained a small bath.

Moira waited at the foot of the stairs. "It needs a lot of work." She dusted her hands and frowned. "Lots of work and lots of money. You'd do better to find a more modern place."

"Yes, but it wouldn't have the same meaning. No basement?"

"Basement? Oh, you mean cellar. Too many bogs around. Unless a place is built on rock you'd just have an unwanted cistern under the house."

Nodding, Tula walked to the door. "I guess I should ask Rory to call the estate agent."

"At least think about it for a day or two. Rory might have ideas on how much the work would cost. You'd have to fix the roof first. You don't have to thatch it. Thatch is dear. Anyway, work out the repair costs first. Last I knew, the owners wanted double the value. I'm sure they thought a rich American would snap it up."

"I'm American, but rich? No. Still, I like the potential of it. It would give me a link to my father."

"Tula, it's too small for a B&B, or even a restaurant. Kilconon isn't on the main road. Kerry gets most of the tourists. A few make it to Dingle, but Kilconon? It's no place for business. If I didn't sell online, my shop wouldn't do enough business to pay for anything. The few tourists who come, do so on a referral from B&Bs in Dingle or with a few guides. Connor usually sends his clients here if they have an interest in such items."

"I could add on or build an annex," Tula continued ignoring Moira's protests. "With the right PR I could make it a destination."

Moira sighed. "I doubt you're listening to me. In any case, my cottage and Mohr house were rebuilt after the war. When Brendan left, he sent money home and his mam used it to modernize the place. It's too bad she didn't put on a new roof. None of the local cottages are original anymore. They're much too dear for the locals. Only developers, Euros, and Brits can afford to do those things."

"I understand your concerns and will think about them. I'll need a business plan, and I'll talk with Rory about repairs, and then the estate agent. Don't worry, Moira, I won't do anything rash."

Tula locked the door and they strolled back to Kilconon to return the key.

* * * *

As they walked, Moira brooded, depressed and angry that Tula refused to see reason. She'd waste her money on Mohr Cottage, and for what? Nothing. The Mohrs died out with Brendan's death. No son remained to carry on the name. Any wealth Tula had should go to her children, unless she died before having any. In that event, the Clares would inherit. The Irish law would ensure that.

Tula needed a will. Moira pondered how to broach the matter. She didn't want her to think the Clares only valued her for the money. If Tula did, she'd leave it to her friends or charity. Father Donnelly would want her to leave it to the church. What a muddle.

Moira had too much respect for money to see her cousin waste it. She pinned her hopes on Ewan. He had to charm Tula into marrying him. No woman could resist him for long. Once they married, Tula would abandon such foolishness, Ewan would see to that.

With the church jumble sale tonight, she might have an opportunity to nudge Tula in the right direction.

When they returned the key, Tula stopped to talk with Rory. "Do you know what the owners want for the place?"

"No, but likely too much. Property hereabouts commanded top

dollar for a while, but not of late. It depends on the owner's need to sell. I can try to find out, but best not to mention you're an American until they name a price."

"Would you? I'd appreciate it. I was thinking of a B&B."

Rory laughed. "In Kilconon? Not likely. There's nothing to bring tourists here."

"That's what Moira said, but you're both wrong. The area, the Dingle Peninsula, attracts tourists. I can make my B&B a destination for discriminating travelers. Anyway, all I'm doing right now is asking what it would cost. I also need to know about roof repairs. Then, if the costs of those two things are manageable, we can move ahead."

Shaking her head, Moira sighed with a glum expression on her face. "She won't listen, Rory. She's as stubborn as any Clare."

He looked from Moira to Tula. "A Clare, eh? I'll see what I can ferret out, but don't get your hopes high."

"Thank you, Rory, I appreciate that."

He grinned at her and looked wistfully at Moira. "Business is slow just now, so why not join me for a cuppa?"

Looking to Tula, Moira then nodded. "After all the dust we stirred up at Mohr House, I could use one."

Rory locked his store and they adjourned to the Kilconon Arms. "Tea for three, Jenny," he said as they entered. They sat near the fireplace and waited.

"So," Rory said to Tula. "I'm guessing you like Kilconon?"

"I love it. The scenery soothes the eyes, no pollution, little traffic, and the people speak to you. Moira's a great cook. To have cousins and Mohr Cottage is more than I ever dreamed."

"Some would say you don't ask much, but I agree, especially Moira's cooking." He smiled at Moira and she blushed. "I plan to sample it tonight at the church dinner."

Jenny arrived with the tea and a plate of popular currant scones. "The cook baked big batches for tonight, so I figured he wouldn't miss a few."

"Ah, Jenny, you'll spoil us for certain." He gave her a broad smile and she turned bright red.

"You've become quite the ladies' man, Rory," Moira said in a teasing voice.

"They pay me little heed." He sighed and gazed at her with puppy-dog eyes. "Now, if you'd say yes..."

"Too much blarney, Rory." Moira frowned and lowered her eyes.

Rory sighed and rolled his eyes. "You see how she treats me, Miss Mohr?"

"I do indeed. Maybe the church dinner will mellow her."

"Enough, both of you," Moira scolded. "I'm glad Tula will see us at our best. It will be a grand dinner with all the singing and dancing to liven us up. Father Donnelly will fill his poor box for once."

"I look forward to your Irish stew, Moira." Rory licked his lips and then grinned at her.

"It's my best dish, so you should." Moira smiled in satisfaction.

Chapter Fifteen

"NO!" Cassie shouted, tangled in the bed covers.

She struggled to focus. She was in her own bed and not on a lonely beach. Sweat dripped from her face.

"Hey, another dream?" Ian stared down at her. "Are you all right?"

"What? Uh, yes. A replay of that huge bird attacking Tula again." Cassie shuddered and pulled the comforter close.

"How long is she going to stay in Ireland?"

"She didn't say. She's found some cousins and her dad's old home."

"Either she'd better come home, or figure out who or what that bird represents."

"You're telling me?" A hysterical laugh came from Cassie. "Leah's worried too."

Ian hugged her close. "If past history is any guide, you'll have to identify what that bird represents."

"I know, but we haven't anything to go on except my dream and what Leah sees in the cards. There's only Tula and that awful bird."

"Do you want a cup of tea? It might help you sleep."

"No, I'm okay now." Cassie snuggled down, determined to sleep. "Thanks, Ian. Just having you here helps a lot."

"I love you, honey. I only wish I didn't feel so helpless."

"At least you don't call me a kook."

"No way, I know better. You saved my life and Ted Muccino's. I couldn't doubt you after that. Try to sleep, sweetheart." He tucked the covers around Cassie.

She made an effort to follow his advice, but sleep remained elusive. As the sky lightened, she finally slept.

The next morning as Cassie finished the breakfast dishes, the phone rang.

"Cassie? Leah. Have you heard from Tula?"

"No, nothing. Have you?"

"No, and I'm worried."

"I had … had another dream last night. Nothing new, just more of the same. Tula's under some sort of threat. Someone wants her dead." Cassie shivered as the dream image of the horrific bird rose in memory. "Do you…. Have you any idea what the bird represents?"

"None, but the cards confirm she has an enemy. Someone wants her out of the way, but I've no idea for what reason."

The thought terrified Cassie. "Love or money. Those are the usual reasons. Love could be jealousy, unrequited love, revenge, or she represents a threat to her enemy's loved one."

"Revenge triggered the threats to both Ian and Ted," Leah said. "But no one in Ireland knew Tula and her father left so many years ago, I can't see revenge."

"Yeah, it doesn't seem likely. That leaves love and money. Money is obvious. Tula may not be rich, but she is well off by most standards. The Tearoom alone must represent at least two hundred thousand or more, and property in Italian Village has escalated in value."

"Sounds like a cool million to me, and that doesn't include any other investments she might have. That's more than enough to tempt someone. I wish we knew more about these cousins of hers."

"Didn't she say Moira… Moira Clare runs an online business? She sells sweaters or some such. I'll do a search on my break today and see what I can find."

"Sounds good to me. Let me know what you discover. I'll send Tula another email. I wish we had a phone number for her."

"So do I. I have to get ready for work. I'll call later when I learn something. Bye."

* * * *

Later at the library, when traffic eased off, Cassie searched for *Moira Clare*. As always, pages of hits or near hits came up. She slogged through them until she found one located in Ireland. The pictures of the sweaters intrigued her. Anything but traditional, she could see why Tula liked them. She made a note of the email address and then called Leah.

"I found the cousin. She sells unusual sweaters and lists an email address."

"We can try it, but we need to be careful how we word the message. It might be best if we asked her to tell Tula to contact us."

"Okay, I can do that. Let me know if you hear from Tula. I'll send the cousin an email."

Cassie disconnected and called up Moira's website. She hit *Contact Me* and keyed a message in the comment space.

```
    Please   ask   Tula   Mohr   to   contact   Cassie
McLeod   or   Leah   Muccino   on   an   urgent   matter.
Thank you.
```

Hoping this Moira Clare would pass the message to Tula, Cassie signed off and leaned back in her chair. So far, neither she nor Leah had learned anything about the raven. They had only had one message each from Tula. Maybe she was having so much fun she forgot to check her email. Or…

Chapter Sixteen

At seven that evening, Tula, Moira, and Ewan walked to the large brick building behind Rory's store. Several cars and trucks were parked nearby. Tula glimpsed Connor's van among them.

Moira carried a large basket with her Irish stew and several items for the jumble sale. "Ewan, take Tula and introduce her to people. I'll give the sale things to Jenny and add my dish to the supper table."

The village hall surprised Tula as she surveyed the large open space. Kilconon appeared too small to support such a grandiose place. Pillars supported the tall ceiling and broke the expanse into sections. The end of the building to the right held tables piled high with various goods, while to the left, covered dishes and baskets sat on tables closest to the wall. Just in front of them stood several rows of empty tables with folding chairs.

She watched as Rory Doyle chatted with Jenny from the pub and another man. Perhaps Rory was interested in Jenny. He'd never said anything. If he married Jenny, would he still help Moira? Her cousin stared at the group with a pained expression.

Moira set her basket on the food table and removed the pot of stew.

"Come with me, Cousin." Ewan reached for Tula's arm.

She ignored his hand. "Lead the way."

He shrugged and grinned at her. "Who haven't you met so far?"

An animated group entering drew Tula's attention. Father Donnelly greeted the Kellys and Connor Kehoe. That made eight people she knew. She hadn't seen Connor or the Kellys since the boat trip.

"I see my American friends, and I want to say hello. They'll be leaving soon." She moved toward them leaving Ewan to stare after her.

"Geneva, Jerome, how nice to see you," Tula said when she reached them. Geneva's glad smile pleased her.

"When Connor suggested coming, I said yes,'" Geneva replied. "The pubs are nice, but Jerome always has a Guinness too many."

"Now, honeybun, that's not so. Good evening, Miss Mohr."

Connor and Father Donnelly nodded to Tula. "Good of you to join us, Miss Mohr," Father Donnelly said. "The church needs all the support we can muster. It's nice to see visitors come, especially from overseas. I can promise you a good meal and some lively entertainment later. Have you seen the items in the jumble sale?"

"Not yet, we've just arrived," Tula responded.

"Come, let me show you some of what we have." Father Donnelly led the way, and Tula and the Kellys trailed after.

"Have you ever been to one of these?" Geneva whispered.

"No, but I hear it's special," Tula replied. "I guess it's like the church fundraisers we have in the States. Moira said the local pub provides a ham. She brought an Irish stew."

Father Donnelly stopped at the first row of tables covered with assorted goods. Several sweaters, knitted and crocheted hats, shawls, throws, and assorted bric-a-brac met her gaze. Another table held watercolors, prints, a few paintings, and books. The variety amazed her. Stickers and tags provided prices.

"I'm sure you'll find something you fancy," Father Donnelly said. "The ladies work hard to provide items for our sale."

Geneva and Tula browsed among the goods. The knitted goods drew Geneva's attention, and Tula watched as she sorted through the sweaters and hats.

Jerome looked with longing toward the tables across the room loaded with dishes of food. "I'll mosey along, honeybun, and see what they have to eat."

"Oh, Tula, look at this." Geneva held up a shawl in purple and mauve. "It's so soft." She draped it over her shoulders.

"It's lovely, Geneva. It would make a special souvenir of Ireland. Besides, it's most likely hand knit and not imported from China."

Tula moved to the table with the pictures and books. Among the offerings, she saw paintings of the church, several scenes of the beach, a few of beehive huts, farms, and even abandoned cottages. One looked a lot like Mohr Cottage. It had the same green door, gray stone walls, and even a half-fallen thatched roof. Enchanted, she looked at the price. She took it to the lady with the cash box and paid for it.

"Do you know the artist?" she said to the woman.

"Oh yes, a local gentleman painted most of the pictures. He sells a lot to tourists."

"I'd like to contact him about doing a painting for me, say in a few months."

The woman handed her a card. "He leaves these in case anyone asks."

Tula glanced down at the card. *Michael O'Brien, Dingle Artist.* An address and phone number followed. "Thank you, this will do."

Geneva bought the shawl and several other items. The cash lady put them in a plastic bag.

They then rejoined Jerome, who now sat at one of the empty tables close to the food table. He looked at Geneva's bags. "I hope you'll remember we pay for extra luggage."

"She can always mail the packages home," Tula said. Geneva gave her a grateful smile.

Father Donnelly rang a large bell. "We don't want the hot dishes to get cold. We have wonderful offerings and a Kilconon ham as well. So fill you plates and let us eat, but first, let's ask the Lord's blessing on us all."

The people clustered around the vacant tables and bowed their heads. After Father Donnelly's brief prayer, they descended on the food. Jerome was among the first. Tula and Geneva waited until the first group passed and then joined the line.

Tula didn't recognize all the dishes, but she saw Moira's stew, a shepherd's pie, some cabbage dish, plenty of potatoes, mushy peas, cheeses, and bread. The sliced ham sat in a place of pride at the far end. She took a sample of most things, but left the soggy peas and cabbage dish.

Jerome had saved them places, and they joined him. Connor followed and pulled out the chair next to Tula.

"It's nice to see you again," Connor said to her. "How do you like Kilconon?"

"Very much. It's all my father claimed. I'm thinking of buying Mohr Cottage."

Connor smiled and then frowned. "A bit of a ruin that. You might want to invest in one that's not derelict."

"Then it wouldn't have the family history. No, I want Mohr Cottage."

"Have you talked with the estate agent yet?"

"Not so far. I've only seen the place. I've no idea what the owners want for it."

"I'd advise letting Rory act for you. If the agents catch a whiff of a rich American interested in the cottage, the price will double overnight." He grinned at her, sharing the truism.

"Thanks, Rory said the same thing. I might do that. Moira thinks I'm an idiot."

"Given the property, she has a point, but I understand family roots. We Irish prize our roots." His smile said he understood.

* * * *

Moira gritted her teeth as she watched Connor hover over Tula. They exchanged smiles, and Tula laughed at something he said, sharing a closeness she envied. She glared at them both. If only Tula would focus on Ewan, but he flirted with Jenny instead.

Sighing, Moira was determined to break up that cozy conversation. She fixed a plate of scones and cream and carried it to Tula. "I thought you'd like these. I added a bit of cinnamon especially for you."

"Thank you, Moira. I was planning to get some." Tula took one of the scones and slathered it with plenty of cream. "Irish cream is so rich."

"Our cows feed on good Irish grass," Connor said with a grin.

"We're going to have singing and maybe even a jig or two," Moira added. "I promised to help organize it. I'm sure you and your friends will enjoy it." She hurried off toward a vacant area beyond the tables.

* * * *

"Are those as good as they look," Geneva asked, staring at Tula's scone with longing.

"Of course," Tula answered. "Have the other one. I love them, but I've eaten way too much tonight. I even left a little cream."

Geneva took the scone, split it, and spread the remaining cream over it. Finished, she bit into it.

Once the scones were eaten, they trailed after the other people and pulled chairs up in a sort of semicircle around a group of men with musical instruments. Tula recognized a bodhrán, a set of Irish pipes, a tin whistle, and a fiddle. The group began with an Irish jig and several older people got up and danced. They put the Riverdance folks to shame. One old lady kicked up her heels with such abandon, Tula feared she might fall or suffer a heart attack. When the spirited dance ended, the dancers sank onto the waiting chairs and fanned themselves.

The quartet switched to some folk tunes. Tula didn't recognize most of them, but then they launched into "The Wild Colonial Boy," and everyone joined the chorus. In the midst of singing, a sudden cramp struck her. Her skin grew clammy and her heart raced. Her rebellious stomach threatened to erupt. Panicked, she looked for the "Ladies."

She stumbled to her feet and headed to the restroom near the front of the hall. Hurried footsteps sounded behind her as Geneva joined her. Together, they bolted toward the "Ladies."

Inside, she took one stall and Geneva the next. She just made it to the W.C. Bent over, she deposited the contents of her supper in the commode. She heaved, heaved again, and heaved once more. Gasping for breath, she couldn't imagine her stomach held anything else. Her mouth tasted vile. She reached up and pulled the cord to flush away the mess. From the sounds next to her, Geneva suffered a similar fate.

"Are you okay?" Tula gasped. Her stomach tried to settle as weakness made her legs wobbly.

"Uh, I … I think so. There can't be anything left."

Tula heard the W.C. flush. She went to the faucet and rinsed her mouth. It eased the horrible, bitter taste. "Rinse your mouth; it helps."

Geneva, red faced from her exertions, joined her at the basin and did so. After several rinses, she looked at Tula. "What did we eat?"

"I don't know. Nothing stands out. Maybe the cream had sat out too long."

"Are we the only ones?" The color faded from Geneva's face to leave it ashen.

"So far, I don't see anyone else here. I'll ask Moira. Maybe she knows. I wouldn't wish this on anybody."

Tula wondered if she looked as pale as Geneva. She took her friend's arm to make sure she didn't fall or stumble. Cassie's warnings surfaced and Tula wondered, had anyone meant mischief? Surely, Geneva and Jerome had no enemies. No more did she. Potlucks always carried the risk of food poisonings. Maybe others were sick too.

Chapter Seventeen

When Tula and Geneva left the restroom, a tenor voice filled the hall with a haunting ballad. As they walked, Tula craned her neck to see who sang. When they neared their seats, she recognized Rory Doyle. She marveled at his voice as he sang "Danny Boy." She'd never heard it performed with more feeling. Transfixed, she stood until the last notes faded.

Several older people wiped their eyes. Connor glanced up as she slid onto her empty chair.

"Are you all right? I considered sending Moira after you. You look a wee bit pale."

"I feel pale, sort of washed out. I guess too much rich food can do that, or else I've picked up a tummy bug." She managed a weak smile.

"Geneva too?" He looked puzzled.

"Yeah, I think maybe it was that cream. Maybe it had turned."

He frowned and studied her face. "No one else seems to have been affected." Tula had no answer.

A wan Geneva leaned toward Connor. "I hate to ask," she whispered, "but could you take Jerome and me back to Mrs. Kennedy's? I'm feeling a bit queasy."

"Of course, I'll bring the van to the door." Connor patted her hand and rose. He spoke briefly to Father Donnelly and left.

The priest approached them with a worried look. "Ladies, Connor said you weren't feeling well. I hope it wasn't anything from dinner."

"I don't know," Tula replied. "Everything tasted so good, I had to sample it all. I might have overdone it." She hated to cause the poor man any concern. It wouldn't do his jumble sale any good if tourists took ill.

"Jerome always warns me to eat light when we travel," Geneva

108

added.

Connor returned and looked to Tula. "Can I drop you at Moira's?"

"No, but thanks anyway. I think I'll have some weak tea to settle myself."

"I'll get it," Father Donnelly said and hurried off.

"I'll say good night then." Connor's look of concern remained. He ushered the Kellys out the door.

Father Donnelly returned with a steaming cup of tea. "I asked Sarah to make it weak. If you need anything, let me know."

Tula nodded and took the cup, grateful for his concern. She sipped the hot tea with care. It went down easily and her stomach relaxed a bit. The musicians played a few more tunes and then folks began to slip away.

At first, Tula didn't see either of her cousins among the departing people. Then, Moira joined her.

"I saw you with your friends and didn't want to bother you."

"I'm sure Geneva would have enjoyed talking with you. Unfortunately, something we both ate didn't agree with us. I'm afraid we left dinner in the W.C."

Moira stared at her with wide, dark eyes. "Were you ill?"

"I'll say. Too much rich foods or maybe that cream had gone off." Tula grimaced at the memory.

"I didn't see or hear of any others getting sick. Could you have picked up something elsewhere, perhaps on that boat trip with Connor?"

"I doubt it. Why wouldn't that have hit us earlier?" Tula studied Moira's face, seeking something, but unsure of what. Jerome hadn't been affected at all.

"Strange, but traveling is a disruption to the system. When we get home, I can fix some stomach powders I use. Are you all right now?"

"Weak and washed out, like this tea, but otherwise fine. It seems to be helping."

"Will you be able to walk home? If not, maybe Rory can drop us there, or Ewan can get the car."

"No, no, I'm fine," Tula protested. "The fresh air is all I need."

Moira looked unconvinced. "I'll gather my pot and things, and find Ewan."

She left and Tula finished her tea. She and Geneva hadn't eaten all the same dishes. They had both sampled Moira's stew and the shepherd's pie. Geneva had tried the peas and that cabbage dish. She hadn't liked either. They had both had a scone with cream, although Tula had used most of the cream.

She took her empty cup to the service table and looked for Moira. She saw no sign of Ewan. Most likely he had gone off with Jenny. Moira approached with her basket and shawl.

"I can't find Ewan anywhere," she said, her annoyance clear.

"Don't worry, Moira, he knows where home is. I'm ready to hit the sack."

"Of course, I'm sorry. How thoughtless of me. Are you sure you can walk to the cottage?"

"Yes, I'm sure."

When they reached the hall door, Father Donnelly stood there. "I believe this is yours, Miss Mohr." He handed her Michael O'Brien's painting.

"Thank you. I'd be sorry to lose it. I've had a lovely evening and enjoyed the jumble sale."

"In spite of being ill?" Worry lined his round face.

"Even so. If I hadn't come, I'd have missed the music and my painting. Rory Doyle has a magnificent voice."

"Indeed, I'm glad he sings in our choir. Too few have such powerful, rich voices. We'll have the unsold items on sale tomorrow, so feel free to return and buy a gift or two."

"I will, goodnight."

He held the heavy door open and then closed it behind them after they left.

The sun had set, but light still lingered in the sky. It amazed Tula how long twilight lasted and how early dawn came. Exhausted, she expected to sleep well tonight.

She and Moira walked in silence to the cottage. The fresh air revived her and cleared her head. When they reached the cottage, Moira unlocked the door and went to the kitchen.

"Would you like a cup of tea or some warm milk?" Moira offered.

"Tea sounds good, but make mine weak with a little honey. Honey

110

always settles my stomach."

Within a few minutes, they sat at the kitchen table and sipped the steaming tea. Moira had made Tula's a pale brown. The honey took any edge from the tea. She studied Moira wondering how to begin.

"Could anyone have doctored the cream or the scones?"

"The Kilconon Arms supplied the scones. Everyone ate them and no one else took sick."

"What about the cream?"

Moira looked thoughtful. "Most didn't use cream. I suppose it's possible. I'm not sure who prepared it."

"It seems strange that only Geneva and I fell ill."

"Indeed, it does. I've no answer for you, Cousin. Once we had an outbreak of some virus or other and it hit the old ones and the infants hard, yet left most of us untouched. If you want, I can ask who fixed the cream."

"Please, do. I can't imagine anyone in Kilconon hating me enough to make me sick."

"I see your point." Moira paused a moment. "Perhaps Jenny or one of the others resented Ewan's interest in you."

"I don't believe that. I've given him no encouragement. He's too young and reckless for me."

Moira sighed. "He is that. Still, others view things in a different light. You never know. There's also Connor. I'm sure one or two have designs on him."

"Connor?" Blinking, Tula stared at her. "He seems a fine man, but he's shown no romantic interest in me."

"He spent the entire evening with you," Moira said, petulance coloring her words.

"With the Kellys and me; they're his clients. Ewan makes a more likely candidate than Connor." Studying her cousin's face, Tula wondered if Moira was jealous.

She finished her tea and rinsed the cup in the sink. "I'm for bed."

"That's unfair, Tula. We're family. In Ireland, kin matter. Your attitude may have annoyed him; he's not used to any woman not responding to him, but he would never hurt you." Moira cleared away the tea things. "You should ask Connor why the Garda take such an interest in him. Good night, Cousin. I'll wait up a bit for Ewan."

Climbing the stairs to her room, Tula found Moira's bitterness surprising. What had she meant about Connor? Too tired to ask, she would leave it all until tomorrow. The sudden illness troubled her, especially after the falling boulder and Cassie's warning. The boulder had been an accident, hadn't it? Rory said rocks fell all the time. Yet that one had just happened to fall as she walked by that spot.

Then, there was Geneva. Why had she also suffered nausea? Instinct pointed to the cream, but who had doctored it and why? Moira had handed the plate to Connor, and he had passed it to her. She couldn't see how he could have added anything. Moira wouldn't want to make her sick. Someone had a reason to frighten her, but who?

Tula tossed for a long time unable to sleep. Who? Who and why? The litany kept running through her mind. Tomorrow she'd go back to the jumble sale and see what she could learn.

Chapter Eighteen

The following day, with Tula still abed, Moira checked her website for orders and messages. She found no orders and only one message. When she read it, she groaned. Tula's friends wanted to talk to her. Moira couldn't think why. Perhaps some problem had arisen with Tula's business. She prayed it wasn't anything to cause Tula to leave. However, better to wait and see what transpired.

Last night when Tula was sick, Connor made much over her, but then the Kellys wanted to leave so he had left early to take the tourists to their B&B. Moira shook her head. Seeing him fussing over Tula enraged her. Yet, she had no wish to see her cousin dead just now or to leave Kilconon, taking her money with her. If only Ewan would convince the woman to marry him. No woman could resist him. He had only to ask.

For now, she could sell her store, but who would buy it? Her debt with Rory kept growing. At some point, even he would have to cut off her account. With Ewan, every pound flowed out like water rushing downhill after torrential rain.

An abyss yawned before her. The sales of her sweaters had dropped off precipitously, and Ewan spent more money than she made. Her savings had evaporated, but Tula's arrival had given her fresh hope. Unfortunately, the American ignored her hints and offered no help. Instead, she rambled on about that derelict Mohr House. It pained Moira to imagine such a useless waste of money.

Her one extravagance was that cursed automobile. Ewan had to get rid of it. He did nothing to pay for it and wanted more money instead. She had to be firm and make him return it.

Footsteps sounded on the stairs. Moira logged off and shut down the computer. She met Tula at the bottom of the stairs.

"Good morning, Cousin. How are you feeling?" To Moira, she looked a little off.

"Much, much better. I slept well. I thought I might check my email and revisit the jumble sale."

"How about breakfast first?"

"You're on. I'm so hungry I could eat three Irish breakfasts."

"We'll start with two eggs and two rashers. With toast and tea, that should do. You don't want to eat too heavily after last night. You can use the computer while I'm fixing breakfast."

"Thanks. The eggs sound great."

Moira adjourned to the kitchen while Tula logged on to her email account in Moira's office. She found a message from Cassie.

```
    Please, stop these dreams. The vengeful
bird frightens me. It means to kill you. You
must find out who your enemy is. Please. Only
you can help us both.
    Love, Cassie
```

Tula remembered only too well Cassie's tale of depression after Ellie Latham died because Cassie hadn't called the police. Her dreams of a deadly rabbit and Ian McLeod plunged her into the search for a vengeful killer, solved only with Tula and Leah's help. That would-be murderer matched Ewan Clare for arrogance and a blatant disregard for others.

Leah's involvement with Ted Muccino brought Cassie more threatening dreams just as she prepared to marry Ian. Those dreams of the cobra led to another self-appointed executioner. Only quick thinking by Ted, with Leah's help, stopped the man.

Now it appeared to Tula that Cassie's current dreams meant someone wanted her dead or gone. She hoped it was the latter. In any event, to help Cassie and end the dreams, she had to discover what or whom the bird symbolized.

"Tula," Moira called. "Breakfast is ready."

* * * *

Once finished with a filling breakfast, Tula said goodbye to Moira and walked to the village hall to check out the jumble sale. She had no idea what she sought, but someone and something had definitely made her and Geneva ill last night. Tula couldn't imagine why anyone would want to hurt Geneva. Given the "accident" on the beach, she concluded she was the likely target, but still couldn't fathom why.

When Tula reached the village hall, a middle-aged woman with dark hair streaked with white was just unlocking the door. "Come for the sale?" she said to Tula.

"Yes, I didn't have time last night to see it all, what with dinner and the entertainment."

"Glad to have you here and may your find many things to buy. The money goes to St. Bridgit's, our church, you know. I'll be here by the door if you need aught." The woman smiled and placed the gray metal box she carried on a table adjacent to the door.

The food tables and chairs had been removed, leaving only the jumble sale tables with their varied goods. Uncertain what she expected to find, Tula walked along the tables of various craft items, collectibles, sweaters, and other miscellany. She thought Moira's sweaters and herbs were at the end of one aisle. She soon came to the pictures by the artist who did watercolors and some oils, mostly in small and even miniature form. She picked up a few of the miniatures—the church, the pub, and a stone bridge over the stream.

She gasped when she saw a larger one depicting the beach and steep cliff side with a massive boulder poised at the top. A flock of seagulls circled about the cliff.

"Beautiful, isn't it?" an older man at her elbow said.

Tula assumed he must be close to a well-preserved sixty in a tweed coat and heavy cord trousers. He wore a navy turtleneck sweater. The rich aroma of his pipe tobacco surrounded him like a halo around his silvery hair.

"Yes, I've seen that very spot. That boulder, or one very like it, almost hit me when it fell to the beach."

"Sorry I am to hear that, and lucky you are to be here. It's sad how the landscape we think unchanging is anything but. Nature is restless this year. They say the sea is rising. Someday it may cover England." He smiled with satisfaction and drew on his pipe.

"Then Ireland would be at risk, too."

"The good lord has plans for us. When the ice melts, Ireland will rise above the waters. You'll see."

Tula smiled at his confidence, and was a bit surprised at his vehemence against England. "Perhaps I should be glad I plan to stay then."

"Indeed you should, Miss Mohr. I'm Michael O'Brien. Glad to see you like my work."

"Yes, I bought the one of Mohr House last night, and I have these miniatures. I'd also like the beach picture, to remind me of that boulder." A slight shiver shook her.

"I'll take these to Mrs. Devlin to hold for you. These days it is especially nice to meet an art lover, particularly one with so discerning an eye." He paused and surveyed Tula with a critical eye, making her glad she'd chosen to wear the teal jumpsuit and the silver necklace.

"Umm... You have a striking, somewhat exotic presence. You're facial structure is superb, and the skin tones—my fingers itch for my brushes. Perhaps later, if you would consider posing for me, I would be honored."

"I as well, Mr. O'Brien." Tula stared at him a moment, flattered by his compliment, but uncertain what he really wanted. Shaking off her doubts, she released the pictures to him.

"Good, I'll be in touch about that portrait. Unfortunately, I have an appointment and must leave, but glad I am to have made your acquaintance." He gave a slight bow and strolled off, pictures in hand, to the hall entrance.

Tula watched him depart, intrigued. Something whispered to her that Michael O'Brien wanted something from her beyond a mere picture. She looked forward to seeing more of him and posing for her portrait.

Continuing down the aisle, she soon reached Moira's table. Several beautiful sweaters remained, and a variety of herb packets, each with a small tag attached identifying the contents and directions for use. She saw ground willow bark, dried willow leaves, powdered Queen Anne's lace, rosemary, and an assortment of others. She knew a bit about herbs and used some in her cooking. She also knew a few carried real danger, such as foxglove and henbane.

It appeared highly likely she had found the source of the sudden nausea she and Geneva had suffered. However, that only meant anyone at the dinner could have used any of the packet contents—but Moira and Ewan had to be at the top of the list. It pained her to think either of her cousins might have wanted to frighten or incapacitate her. The dose hadn't been strong enough to kill. Or would it, if she had eaten both scones?

Locked in her unpleasant thoughts, Tula approached the woman sitting by the door. "I think you're holding some pictures for me."

"Yes, indeed. Mr. O'Brien left them here with a sales slip. He gave you a ten percent discount since this is our last day. I've put them in a carrier bag for you."

"Thanks." Tula pulled out her wallet and counted out the Euros, glad she had stopped by the bank to change some money.

"You're a visitor to Kilconon," the woman said as she took the money.

"Yes, my father, Brendan Mohr, was born here, so I was curious to see his birthplace. It's my first visit to Ireland."

The woman gave her an odd look. "Brendan Mohr? That was years ago. Let me see... I think I was twelve that year. It was the same year my brother Grady married Maeve Clare. May she and all the Clares be forever cursed."

"The Clares?" Tula stared at the woman, wondering the cause of the outburst, but before she could ask, the woman jumped to her feet.

"Pardon me, I see Mrs. Dunn and must speak with her." The woman hurried over to Father Donnelly's housekeeper.

"Perhaps we can talk another time," Tula called after her.

Suspecting that Moira would begin to wonder where she was, Tula picked up her packages and left. Outside, she saw Connor's van parked by Rory's store. She approached and found Connor and Rory deep in conversation.

"Morning, Mr. Doyle, Connor. I've just been to the jumble sale."

"Glad to see you've made a few purchases," Connor said. "I'm sure Father Donnelly will appreciate it."

"So, what struck your fancy," Rory asked, staring at the bags Tula carried.

"More pictures by Michael O'Brien," she responded. "He had one of the beach and the boulder before it fell, or one like it."

"He's talented," Rory observed. "Mostly, he sets his price too high for us folks. Most of his work goes to tourists."

"Why not?" Connor said. "They can afford it. He could go anywhere and do well."

"Too true," Rory replied with a broad grin. "Still, I wouldn't mind having one of the town or my farm."

"What's he like?" Tula prompted.

"A loner for the most part," Connor said. "We see him at the pub now and then, or when he's out sketching. He doesn't mix much."

"He asked if I'd pose for him," Tula said.

"No wonder there. He's an eye for beauty, especially for those who are out of the ordinary. You more than qualify, especially with your Irish silver."

"I'll take that as a compliment, Captain Kehoe."

"It was meant as one," Connor said. "Now, Rory and I have a proposition for you."

Tula raised an eyebrow at that. "Haven't had one since I arrived." That brought a smile from both men.

"The Irish are falling behind," Connor said. "No, Rory and I agree you must see the Cliffs of Moher. At present, I'm between clients, so we thought tomorrow would be the day to remedy that. We'd like to take you and Moira with us. I'm sure she could stand a day without Ewan to worry her. What do you say?"

The Cliffs of Moher. Tula wondered yet again whether the fabled cliffs had any ties to her family. "Yes, I want very much to see them. Geneva and Jerome raved about them. I'm not so sure about Moira. She worries so about her shop."

"She needs to get away," Rory insisted. "She looked so down last night during dinner. Please, do your best to persuade her."

His concern for Moira and his almost pleading tone made Tula realize the two men had more in mind than just a tourist visit. She was curious to discover exactly what. Pursing her lips, she considered the trip and her stubborn cousin.

"I want to go and with a little urging, perhaps we can pry Moira lose. It's too good an invitation to pass up with two handsome men to lend Moira and me their arms."

Rory looked relieved and Connor gave her an approving smile.

"I'll pick you both up around eight tomorrow morning," Connor said. "How about a ride to Moira's with those packages?"

"You're on. Shall we go?"

Connor put the paintings in the van while Tula climbed in the front passenger seat. Five minutes later, he stopped in front of the cottage and got out. He retrieved the paintings and carried them to the door.

"I've a few things to tend to today, so I'll leave you now. I'm looking forward to tomorrow and sharing more of Ireland's wonders with you." He paused a moment and gazed at her with a seriousness that surprised her. "I trust you to persuade Moira. It's important to Rory. He'd like a chance to court her away from distractions."

"Aren't the Cliffs a distraction?" Arching an eyebrow at him, Tula grinned.

"No, she's seen them before. It'll give him more uninterrupted time with her than he's managed for some time. It would please me a great deal if you both came."

Sighing, Tula nodded. "I'll do my best, but you know how stubborn she can be."

"Ah, yes, but I trust your abilities to carry the day. I'll see you both at eight." He tipped his cap and returned to the van.

Tula watch him drive away and then carried her paintings into the cottage. Moira was in the kitchen washing dishes. Pulling out a chair, Tula sat at the table.

"Ready for some tea?" Moira said over her shoulder. Tula nodded, and Moira put on the kettle.

"I ran into Connor in the village. He offered to take us to the Cliffs of Moher."

"Oh?" Moira raised an eyebrow. "I've the shop to mind and sweaters to knit. That trip would take all day."

"It's one place I'm anxious to see. I've been wondering about the name since it sounds like mine."

"Can't say I know about that. The Burren is more interesting to me because of its plants." Moira busied herself fixing the tea.

"If it's near the Cliffs, I'm sure we could stop there too. The trip would do you good, and I'd like the company. I don't know if he has others coming as well, but he said to ask you. We'll have a great time. It will do you good to get away for a day. I hardly saw you last night."

"I don't know your friends and didn't want to interfere. Besides, I had other things to do, what with the sale tables and all."

"Interfere? Why would you think that?" Tula studied Moira's stiff back. She was too much of a loner. It was as if she didn't like people. "The Kellys are nice people, and they enjoyed the evening, that is, until Geneva got sick."

"Strange that," Moira responded. She set the teapot on the table and filled the milk pitcher.

"Yes, it was. I guess we were the only two affected. I'm sure it had to be the cream. Anyway, I would appreciate it if you came tomorrow."

Moira sat opposite Tula and poured herself a cup of tea. "Connor's so focused on that boat of his I'm surprised he has the time."

"He took the Kellys there a few days ago, but they're gone now. I'm looking forward to the trip. So far, I've only seen Dingle, Kilconon, and the puffin island."

Nodding, Moira then sipped her tea. "I suspect going with Connor doesn't hurt either." After a brief pause, she continued. "Do you like him?"

Tula stirred her tea and considered what to say. "He's a fine guide and good with his clients."

"Sure now, he wouldn't be in business long if he wasn't. He can be as charming as Ewan when he wants. I'm sure you discovered that last night. Do you like him?"

"Like?" Tula paused a moment, wondering why her cousin asked that. "What's not to like? He's pleasant and helpful."

Moira laughed, eyes sparkling. "A bit cool, that. Sure now, that's true of all tour guides. How do you find him as a man?"

"I'm not sure what you mean, Moira."

The direct questions made Tula unhappy and suspicious. She'd guessed her cousin was interested in Connor, but couldn't quite believe Moira might be so jealous of her that she would resort to making her sick. She was a relative and a visitor after all.

"He's a handsome devil and broke many hearts before he went to university," Moira continued. "I would not see you hurt, Cousin."

Laughter shook Tula, followed by increasing doubt. "Ah, Moira, he's the consummate guide. He's polite and attentive to all his clients. I've never seen more than that." Tula stared at the milky surface of the tea, still not entirely sure of her feelings for Connor. "I'm a visitor and he knows that. I'll be going soon in another week or two."

"Indeed, but you still haven't answered me, Cousin."

"I find him attractive and intelligent; as anyone would." She had no desire to continue the conversation and resented Moira's persistence.

"True, but faint praise indeed." Moira sighed and continued with stern look. "I'd advise you to watch yourself though. He's in need of money for his boat, and you're a rich tourist. He'd find that irresistible."

"I'm comfortable, but not rich, as you put it." Tula stared at Moira, taken aback by her words. "I'm sure he could find a much better source of money than me."

"Maybe, but you're here. Listen to what he says to you, then tell me he isn't interested in your money."

Tula wanted nothing more than to end this unpleasant conversation. "Come along tomorrow, and you'll see he has no interest in me or my money."

"I'll consider it." Moira took her empty cup to the sink. "Would you like something for lunch?"

"Is it that time? Something light would do."

She had been so certain Moira was jealous over Connor, but now it seemed she was concerned as much about Tula's money and how she spent it.

Chapter Nineteen

The next morning, Connor, in a hopeful mood, parked his van beside Moira's cottage. He knocked at the door and waited. This trip would give him more time with the intriguing Tula Mohr while Rory romanced Moira. With a bit of Irish charm and luck, he might learn what the woman thought of him, and Rory might finally convince Moira to wed him.

Moira opened the door and offered him a welcoming smile. "Good morning, Connor. Tula is upstairs."

"Good day, Moira. Nice weather for our trip."

"Indeed. I'll get her." She went to the stairs and called. "Tula, Connor's here."

Tula descended the stairs with a raincoat over her arm and a daypack. Her brown wool slacks and green tunic reminded him of the hills through which they would pass. Her walking shoes would do well for trekking along uneven, rocky paths.

"Moira, where's your coat?" Tula looked at her cousin with puzzlement. "Connor says we should always take one considering Irish weather."

Sighing, Moira pushed her hair off her forehead. "I ought stay here and make Ewan's breakfast."

Tula rolled her eyes. "He can do for himself for one day. It would do him good."

Connor held his breath. If Moira didn't come, Rory wouldn't either. Rory had to convince Moira to rely on him so she wouldn't continue trying to trap a sea captain instead. Besides, Rory loved her and deserved all the help he could get. Moira's Irish temper made her a difficult one to convince of anything, and few sensible men would want to cope with

Ewan. It was past time for that one to work and fulfill his role as head of the family.

"Moira, don't coddle the boy," Connor scolded. "You need a holiday as much as anyone. How long has it been since you've seen the Cliffs?"

"Years, at least," she said and sighed.

"How about the new visitor centre at the Cliffs? I'll wager you haven't set foot in it."

"Ah, that's so. I've too much to do to waste a day on such things."

"Where's your Irish spirit? Certain I am you'll find new inspiration for your sweaters. Besides, you don't want to spoil my plan to escort the two loveliest ladies in Kilconon on a visit."

Moira smiled, amused. "Now you sound like Ewan. Tula may be a beauty, but no one has called me one in years."

Tula looked from Moira to Connor and back again, as if pondering how to sway Moira. "Connor's right, Moira. Come with us. We'll have a great time, and I'm sure you must know stories about these places Connor doesn't. I want to see and learn about all the fabled sites." She paused a moment. "You said the Burren has plants that only grow there."

"'Tis true," Moira said. "One cannot find some of the beautiful bog orchids anywhere else. Unique herbs grow wild there as well."

"See? All the more reason to come with us. I can carry anything you'd like to collect in my pack."

Connor smiled, but said nothing about the prohibition against collecting plants in the Burren. The government added more restrictions as scientists studied the area. Moira would find out soon enough, but once they were on the road, she'd have no choice but to continue. Rory would be more than happy to console her.

Shifting from foot to foot, Moira, with indecision clearly evident on her face, gazed first at Tula and then at Connor, who smiled back, hoping to encourage her. "All right, a day away won't make much difference the way things are now. I'll get my mac and some bags for herbs. I'll just leave a note for Ewan." She hurried to the kitchen.

In five minutes, she returned with a pack of her own and her brown mac. "Ready when you are."

Connor opened the door, and they trooped out to his van. "I'm putting Tula in front so she can see the scenery better. If you would, Moira, please sit in back."

He helped both women into the vehicle. Rory would sit with Moira. Connor prayed to the Irish fairies to bless them and sprinkle her with love dust. He smiled inwardly, only too aware Rory would need all his powers of persuasion to change her stubborn mind.

"All set, ladies?" Both women nodded.

He drove to Rory's store and parked in front. "I won't be a minute. I'll get some bottled water for us."

* * * *

When Rory followed Connor out of his store, Tula wondered if Connor planned matchmaking. A tartan plaid cap gave him a sporty look, and went well with his brown corduroy jacket. Like Moira, he carried one of the waxed raincoats popular among farmers. He looked handsome in a fresh, hearty way and smiled as he joined them.

Tula winced at Moira's frown as she slid over to make room for Rory. That boded ill for him and any schemes he and Connor had in mind. A man like Rory would be ever faithful and spoil Moira more than she did Ewan. Except for her evident rejection, it would be an ideal match, according to Connor.

"Good day, Moira, Miss Mohr. I hope you don't mind my joining the party. I haven't seen the Cliffs in years. Connor made it sound irresistible."

"He did the same to me," Moira said, one cynical eyebrow raised.

"We're off, then." Connor started the van.

On this drive, Tula had no trouble staying awake and surveying the Irish countryside. On her first trip, she had slept through the journey when jet lag exerted its toll. Today, they passed small fields separated by stonewalls where flocks of sheep and goats grazed. She even glimpsed small herds of cows and pigs. The road passed a mountain—small by U.S. standards—climbed a pass, and then dropped down to the city of Tralee by the ocean. The colorful gardens of the city testified to the mild climate and rich soil. Beyond the city, they soon reached farmland and pastures again.

Gazing over the green fields fenced by fuchsia and stone, Tula tried to decide what in the landscape she missed. Then she realized she had seen only a small number of trees away from the towns.

"Connor, why does Ireland have so few trees?"

"Ah, that's a mystery, and the answer depends on whom you ask," he answered. "Some scientists say early farmers cleared the land as the population grew to plant crops and pasture cattle. Sheep will eat almost anything. So, once a farmer cleared the land and used it for a sheep pasture, trees no longer grew there."

Rory snorted in the backseat. "No, Connor, put the blame where it rightly belongs. It's the English."

Connor grinned at Tula. "You see, Miss Mohr, the Irish blame the English for this as they do for many other things. They ruled Ireland for hundreds of years. They tried to suppress our language and destroy our culture. They stole our trees to build ships and feed their iron mills, or so the story goes. However, they also brought massive change, both good and bad."

"Indeed, but we fought them," Moira interjected. "With a common enemy, the Irish banded together instead of squabbling with each other over land and cattle."

The lively discussion amused Tula and she wanted to keep it going. "But not in Northern Ireland," she said. "The English are still there."

"True." Moira sighed looking downcast. "Sooner or later they'll leave, and we can be one nation again."

Connor laughed and Rory joined him. "The Irish have never been one nation."

"Ah, Connor, sure there's hope," Rory said, a bit breathless. "Still, you can't trust the English, ever. Thieves and liars they were and are. They used our trees to build those ships to steal Spanish gold from the New World, and to fuel their forges to make weapons to use against us." Rory's attitude apparently came as no surprise to Connor.

To Tula, much of this wasn't new. She knew about the Irish clans and the feuds between the Catholics and the Protestants. Having lived in the U.S. for years, she sometimes had to remind herself that her heritage was Irish and African. A cosmopolitan education and wealth made her less tied to any country, even Ireland, and to past injustices than was the case for Rory and Moira. At least the history kept them from boredom.

"I guess you could compare the English treatment of the Irish," Tula said, "to the way European settlers of North and South America acted toward the native populations and the Africans imported as slaves. Americans share the blame with the English. The English and other nations settled the U.S. and Canada. Yet without the lure of gold, would the New World have been settled so quickly?" She expected that to stir the discussion.

Connor laughed, eyes sparkling. "You see, whoever had the largest fleet or the fastest ships commanded the world. You Americans have done that with your military, ships, airplanes, and now those drones."

Not at all happy with this trend of the conversation, Tula groaned. "Don't remind me. At least that 'master of the world' era has ended. So, where were we? Either the Irish destroyed their environment or the English did."

"A bit of both," Connor replied. "However, the English did the most damage. In the nineteenth century, a few English landlords planted trees to make parks for the deer they wanted to hunt. That brought back some forests."

"Humph," Rory snorted. "Indeed, but they took the farmers' land and planted the fields with trees for those 'hunting preserves.' The land clearances are why so many of the Irish went to Canada and America. They lost their land, their way of life, and livelihood."

"Really?" Tula stared at him. "I thought the Irish migrated because of the potato famine. Some disease or other destroyed the potatoes."

"Yes, but the clearances made it much worse. The English always hated the Irish."

"Let's not rehash all that, Rory," Connor said. "We're discussing trees, remember? When we got self-rule, over time, our government began planting trees too, but those efforts also caused problems because they didn't use native species. Now the emphasis is how to reduce the impact of climate change and return to native forests. In any case, much of Ireland's west coast isn't suitable for trees, what with the bogs and the karst of the Burren."

"Karst?" Tula couldn't quite recall what karst was.

"Much of the Burren is made of limestone, great for orchids, but not for trees or agriculture," Connor explained. "When we stop at the visitor center, you'll see the exhibits and learn the history of the area much better than any of us can tell it."

Soon, they arrived at the Burren visitor center and viewed the informative exhibits. Tula enjoyed wandering through the displays and found the pieces on the Burren microclimate fascinating. It had survived even the Ice Age. Moira focused on the vegetation and various orchid varieties. However, she soon turned away and cornered Connor as they left the exhibits.

"Did you know they prohibit taking any plants from the Burren?" Her voice was shrill and accusatory.

"Things change," Connor replied. "I guess too many people were taking the rare ones, so they banned removing any vegetation or stones. I'm sorry, but at least we can still look at them."

Moira gave him a look that would frighten most men. Tula sighed, glad when Rory joined them.

Connor rolled his eyes at Rory, as if to say "I told you so."

"Yes, well, we've still the Burren itself and the Cliffs to see. Let's follow the road and find a few places to stop and view the flora and the megalithic monuments. I'll bring the van to the door." He hurried off to the car park.

Tula decided he was eager to escape Moira's anger and hid a smile. She waited with Rory and a disgruntled Moira for the van. It soon came into view.

Once Connor pulled up and stopped in front of them, he jumped out and hurried around the van toward Tula. Rory, smiling broadly, assisted Moira into the backseat and quickly scrambled in behind her. Connor took Tula's hand and held the van door for her. With an intimate smile, he retained her hand for a moment before he winked at her. An increased awareness of him caused sudden heat to spread through her, even to her toes.

Once on the road again, Connor drove slowly through the interesting and unique landscape. Tula struggled to keep her thoughts on the megalithic remnants she glimpsed from the road. She could understand Moira's attraction to Connor, even though he did not appear to share an attraction for her. Of course, he saw many women among the tourists and had attended an Irish university. Even though he had returned to his roots, Tula guessed he would want more in a wife than Moira could offer.

Neither Rory nor Moira spoke during the drive through the Burren perhaps from lack of interest, irritation on Moira's part, or just lulled by the drive. Connor made no stops.

* * * *

When they arrived at the Cliffs of Moher, Moira and Rory trailed behind Connor and Tula. Moira increased her pace, anxious not to let the others leave them behind. She wanted no personal discussions of the money she owed Rory. Guilt weighed on her almost as much as her determination not to leave Connor and Tula alone.

"Moira," Rory touched her arm. "I've been meaning to talk with you."

She gazed toward Connor and Tula moving ahead at a fair speed. "We should stay close to the others."

"I want a word with you." He lowered his voice. "It's … it's about money."

"Money? What do you mean?" Her first thought was he wouldn't advance her any more. Her second was, now of all times, he would demand repayment of the money she owed him.

Rory sighed as he studied her face. "Things are difficult for you just now, and I want to help you. Perhaps a small loan might make things easier for you."

Breathing a trifle easier, she stared at him, uncertain what to say. "We manage."

Rory shook his head. "Ewan's shown no interest in getting a job. He's a drain on you. Paying his lease payment is too much for you. He should get a job or return the car."

Moira pulled away and looked toward the sea. "Leave Ewan out of this. He's not your problem."

"He is my problem because he's your problem and I care about you. Either let me loan you some money … or … you could marry me." He looked at her with longing.

Marriage to him would ease things, but she didn't love him. Ewan came first. If only Connor showed some interest in her instead of flirting with her cousin. He had a future as more than a farmer, and Ewan needed someone with Connor's strength and ambition.

Frustrated, Moira dug her nails into her palms and moved along the path, hoping to see Connor and Tula. "I've no intention of marrying anyone."

"Not even Connor?" Rory said.

"Connor?" She snorted. "That one's in no hurry to marry anyone. He's too busy with his boat."

"Don't be too certain of that. He seems taken with your cousin."

Staring at the couple ahead as they moved farther away, Moira watched Connor guide Tula along the path and point out various sites. He walked close beside her, and she laughed at something he said. Their easy camaraderie disturbed Moira. It brought back the scene at the church dinner with Connor leaning close to Tula. Anger gripped her.

"I'm sure she'd rather have Ewan," Moira snapped in a waspish voice. "He's younger, handsomer, and far more charming."

Rory threw back his head in laughter and brushed tears from his eyes. "No sensible woman would choose Ewan over Connor. Ewan's a reckless boy who only cares about his next conquest. He has no job, no future. Your cousin has too much sense not to see that. No, Moira, don't place your hopes on Ewan's marrying Tula. She won't have him." Moira made no reply.

Other tourists hurried past them, and they soon lost all sight of Connor and Tula.

"Perhaps some tea would suit," Rory said. "We've a ways to go yet."

Clearly frustrated, Moira nodded.

* * * *

Despite having seen higher cliffs along the California coast and in the Grand Canyon, Tula still found the Cliffs of Moher breathtaking, aided in no small way by the restless ocean at the foot of the cliffs. Connor and Tula strolled along the path to O'Brien's Tower. Rory and Moira were somewhere behind. The tower looked toward the sea, and as they neared it, Tula saw a line of visitors outside waiting for admittance.

"The tower is a short climb, but the seaward view is worth it,"

Connor said. "Shall we?"

Tula nodded, and they joined the short queue. Before long, they reached the entrance. She led the climb up the tower's winding stone steps with Connor close behind. Small openings in the wall provided light and glimpses of the sea. At the top, she gazed out to the water and counted the freighters sailing up the coast.

"Perhaps you'd like to see the Cliffs from the sea," Connor said. He stood close beside her and his warm breath caressed her neck. His nearness and confident masculinity stirred her senses.

"Yes, I'd like that," she replied in a breathless voice.

Tempted to lean back, she resisted. This was too public a place for romance. Other people waited below. With one last look out the window, she turned to descend. "We'd better go."

Connor nodded and led the way. She followed close behind. He took possession of her hand at the bottom of the steps to lead her from the tower. The sun hid behind a cloud for a moment.

"Well, what do you think of the Cliffs, Miss Mohr?" Connor said as they strolled along the cliff top path.

"Tula, remember, Connor." She stressed his name and savored his broad smile. "I'm impressed. They remind me a lot of parts of the Northern California coast, especially since they look west."

"I'm glad to be able to show you your namesake." Connor blue eyes sparked with promises.

Unsettled, she looked away to the people on the path ahead. She saw no sign of Rory or Moira ahead or behind. "I wonder where the others are."

"No surprise there," Connor said. "Rory wanted time alone with Moira. I only hope she'll listen," he said as they continued along the cliff top path.

A gaggle of tourists hurried along the path behind them. The sunshine, the restless sea, and the rocky cliffs provided a feast for the senses. Being with Connor added a touch of romance, although he had said little. She enjoyed their closeness and mild flirtation, but cautioned herself that he probably meant nothing serious. Despite Moira's warning, he hadn't mentioned money.

"After we return to Kilconon, we'll stop at the pub," Connor said.

"However, I thought perhaps you might share a meal with me in my cottage."

Tula stopped and studied his face, wondering where that might lead. Would romance also be in the offing?

"To see your Irish etchings?" She quirked an eyebrow at him.

"Umm, maybe if I were English or American, but no, I have some maps of Ireland I think might interest you, and as an added inducement, I have fresh fish, early peas, and Irish potatoes. I enjoy my own cooking and hope you might too."

The man could cook as well as pilot a boat. The more she learned about Connor, the more intrigued she grew. "Umm, that's too good an offer to refuse. I've never seen your cottage."

His broad smile pleased her, and when he took her arm, she didn't refuse. "Now, I suggest we return to the visitor's center and have some tea and perhaps a cream scone, unless the church jumble sale put you off them."

"You're on. I've no worry anyone here would bother to poison me. As for dinner, that's too good an offer to refuse."

Connor stopped abruptly, a shocked look on his face. "You think that's what happened?"

"I'm certain of it. You know Moira sells herbs and powders. I checked her table at the jumble sale and noticed one packet prescribed for stomach ailments, but with a warning that too much could induce vomiting."

"You think Moira was responsible?"

"I know so few people in Kilconon. No one else would have a reason. As for Moira and Ewan, I'm not sure. Unless someone holds an old grudge against my father." She paused for a moment. "You know they're both short of funds, as Moira keeps reminding me. I suppose it sounds hard-hearted, but I've no intention of subsidizing Ewan's lifestyle or his fancy car. I'd help Moira, but anything I gave her would go directly to Ewan. As it is, I help by paying to stay with them." Tula sighed.

"Umm. Sorry am I to think either might be bent on harm or murder. Although, Ewan is into things frowned upon by the Garda. Perhaps you should consider staying elsewhere."

"I've thought about it, and may yet. I wish she'd stop pestering Ewan to marry me." Tula frowned at the thought. "There's no way in hell I would. She wants me to write a will. I've been thinking about one, a trust for Mohr House. I'm certain she wouldn't like that."

"Does that mean you're considering staying in Ireland?" Connor looked hopeful.

"I could be persuaded." Tula grinned at him. "I'm waiting to see what dinner's like."

* * * *

After rejoining Rory and Moira outside the coffee shop, they returned to the van and Connor began the drive back to Kilconon. Moira looked sulky and said little. Rory, too, was uncharacteristically quiet.

"We have a choice," Connor said. "We can stay on the road toward Kilconon, or we can take a short detour west to the end of the coastal cliff path that runs all the way north to the Visitors Center for the Cliffs. Hag's Head, the beginning or end of the Cliffs, lies just beyond where the path turns east."

"Hag's Head? Not a pretty name," Tula responded.

"Ah, but it's a tale of romance," Rory added. "According to legend, a *cailleach*, witch, or hag, called Mal, fell madly in love with the great Irish hero, Cú Chulainn, a warrior of miraculous strength and power." A born storyteller, Rory paused.

"I remember the tale of the Washer Woman," Tula added.

"Sad as is so often the case, the warrior, with his choice of maidens, wanted none of her. He ran all over Ireland trying to escape her, eventually ending up at the Cliffs of Moher. The love-sick Mal now had him in sight with no way for him to avoid her amorous embrace. However, being a brawny and brainy lad, our hero escaped by jumping from the Cliffs of Moher using the rock pillars as stepping stones.

"The poor, lovelorn wretch, tired from her endless pursuit, was weak and a bit clumsy. She struggled to chase him. However, one false step finished her. She was dashed to pieces against these very cliffs. She fell to her death at Hag's Head, where her blood stained the sea red for miles."

"Ah, but the Morrigan claimed him," Tula said.

"Indeed, she did. The Crow Goddess always demands her due. Heroes know that death, not life, is their reward."

"The Crow Goddess," Tula repeated remembering Cassie's warning. What would a goddess of death and war have to do with her?

"Crow or raven I've heard," Rory responded. "There are tales and tales of the Morrigan. At times, I've wondered if Mal was an incarnation of that deity. Cú Chulainn bested her several times before he died."

"The Morrigan was not a *cailleach*," Moira insisted. "She was the mightiest goddess of all. She also brings visions of the future."

"Ah, so I've heard," Rory said in a troubled voice. "Does she visit you often?"

"I never said she inspired my dreams. Besides, I have no visions now," Moira insisted.

That avowal rang false. Tula gathered Rory didn't believe Moira, and neither did she. Perhaps visions like Cassie's had caused Moira's sudden change of attitude and coldness of late. If so, what had her visions revealed? Tula needed answers, but remained uncertain how best to get them.

Chapter Twenty

After leaving the Hag's Head area, Tula found herself nodding off on the return trip. The fresh air and exercise demanded payment. She had been in Ireland long enough to adjust to the jet lag and the time change, but she had yet to establish a routine or do much in the way of regular exercise. Climbing O'Brien's Tower and strolling along the Cliffs in the sea air had exhausted her. She worried Connor might also be too tired to cook dinner or... The "or" concerned her the most. She was in the mood for a romantic evening with a handsome Irish man with the potential to be a keeper, provided he wasn't just out for a fling... or her money.

She found something compelling about a man so in command of himself and self-assured. That same presence had attracted her to the suave, sophisticated Mario. However, while Connor had flirted a bit, his intentions were not clear. She had no interest in a causal affair.

So far, she hadn't factored in her own heritage. Her Irish father had married her beautiful Somali mother, which gave her hope. The Irish as a race, at least the educated ones, appeared less concerned about race than Americans. In any case, she was proud of her mixed heritage. So far, Connor hadn't shown any signs it bothered him.

When the party reached the Kilconon Arms, they all piled out and entered the warm pub. A peat fire smoldered on the hearth, filling the air with a rich, earthy smell. She and Moira commandeered a table and four chairs while Connor and Rory placed their orders at the bar—a single malt for Tula and Connor, a cider for Moira, and a pint for Rory. The men soon returned with drinks.

"To friends, old and new," Rory said and raised his glass with a broad wink at Tula.

"To friends," the rest echoed.

134

After everyone took their first sip, they settled back to enjoy the fire. Tula suspected that Moira had remained prickly and immune to Rory's pleas. Neither gave any sign of having settled things between them. Rory, ever solicitous of Moira's comfort, took care not to block the warmth of the fire from her.

"Well, Moira, did you enjoy the trip?" Connor said.

"I was disappointed the bloody authorities banned gathering herbs in the Burren, despite what you told me, Connor," Moira berated him, looking not at all happy.

"Umm, sorry about that," he replied, not looking sorry at all. "The government keeps changing the regs, and the bloody EU just compounds those problem. My usual customers don't collect such things. If you give me a list of the plants you want, I'll look for them elsewhere."

Ever the peacemaker, Rory patted Moira's hand. "It's been a long day. What say we order fish and chips or something and have dinner here?"

"I've Ewan to consider, and Tula," Moira responded in a waspish voice.

"Don't worry about me," Tula interjected, only too eager to encourage Moira to stay. "As for Ewan, by this time he's usually found some young thing to pursue. Stay here and eat. No sense standing at a hot stove tonight." Moira looked like she wanted to protest.

"Tula's right, Moira. After all that walking, you deserve to have dinner served," Rory insisted. He motioned to Jenny to take their order. "What's your fancy?"

Moira looked at the board and ordered bangers and mash while Rory opted for a burger and chips. Jenny looked to Connor. He shook his head.

"Tula and I'll be back later. I promised to show her a couple of local maps. Keep our seats warm."

Tula was glad Moira didn't have the power to kill at a glance. Her glare only re-enforced Tula's belief that she had tampered with the scones. Joining Connor, they walked side by side to the exit.

Outside, she drew a deep breath. "Whew. Moira wasn't happy."

"Poor Rory. She's not worth the effort, especially with Ewan dragging along with her." He held the door to the van open for Tula.

"Without Ewan, they might have a chance. Rory really deserves better."

"I agree, but he's loved her since they were children. Loyalty like that should be rewarded." Connor sighed.

"I never would have guessed you're a romantic."

Connor smiled as he pulled into the driveway of a small stone cottage. "Sure now, all we Irish dream. It's better than the reality all too many face. At least I'm working to make my dreams come true."

He came around to the passenger side and opened the door for her. His warm hand enveloped hers as he assisted her from the van. "The Kehoe Manor awaits your presence," he said with a courtly bow.

Connor unlocked the bright blue door and pushed it open so Tula could enter. Pleasant warmth flowed out. Inside, the scent of beeswax and roses perfumed the air. The neat, cozy room surprised her. No clutter or dust lay anywhere. She wondered if he had a cleaning lady and then remembered the *Seabird*. His cottage was as shipshape as his boat.

"Nice," she said. For a moment, she stared at the haunting seascape above the fireplace. She could almost see the wind whipping the breaking waves onto the stony shingle. "I like that painting. Is it by Michael O'Brien?"

"No, a friend painted it." Connor took Tula's things and hung her jacket on a hook by the door. "Now, if you'll excuse me a minute, I'll start our supper and return with glasses of a pleasant Irish white wine."

Tula made a circuit of the room, examining the furniture and the few photographs. The chairs looked comfortable and well used, especially the chintz covered one by the fireplace. The largest photograph was of an older woman, gray haired with a sweet face and eyes like Connor's.

"That's my mother," Connor said on his return and handed Tula a glass of wine. "She died a few years back after a life of hard work and caring for her family. If not for her, I might have become another Ewan."

"Instead, you became a son of whom she could be proud."

"I hope so. We Irish love our mothers. It's tragic Ewan's mam died when he was a mere bairn and Moira raised him. Enough about him, I'd rather talk about you."

"Me?"

"Yes. How did Miss Mohr become Tula?"

She smiled at the question. "Like you, my mother was a big influence on me. She made sure I went to the best schools Europe could offer. Unfortunately, she and my father died when I was in college. After that, I went to the States. I ended up in Columbus, opened my café, and here I am."

"All by yourself? No friends or ... fiancé?"

"Friends, yes. Serious relationships? Umm. Perhaps one, but we broke it off."

"I suspect there's more to the story, but dinner is about ready. The table is set, so if you'll take a seat, I'll bring the food." Connor hurried off to the kitchen.

Tula did as requested. The tableware was real silver in a satin finish and almost glowed, reflecting the light of the candles at both sides of the table. A damask cloth provided the backdrop for a small vase of pink roses. She couldn't imagine a better setting for a little romance.

Soon, Connor returned with two plates of food. Each held a silvery grilled fish, a boiled potato with a generous dollop of yellow butter, and bright green peas. He set one in front of her and placed the other across the table.

"Shall we eat?"

Tula nodded, Connor taking a seat opposite her. The fish, a pleasant white variety dusted with herbs and butter, melted in the mouth. The Irish potato and the early peas provided the rest of the meal, and a little sweetness. She savored every bite.

"Connor, this is delicious. I never would have guessed you would be such a fine chef."

"Good ingredients, a little help from Mrs. O'Brien, the lady who helps me out on occasion, a quick grill, and we have dinner."

"Um, have you had a lot of practice?"

Connor smiled at her with a decided gleam in his eyes. "Some."

"Does that mean there've been many such times," Tula asked, waiting impatiently for the answer.

"Actually, almost none." Connor grinned at her, a gleam in his eyes. "My business takes most of my time. Finding clients takes effort. In any event, finding the right person is difficult."

"You'll have to tell me more about the 'right person.'"

"I will, Miss Mohr, but now we have this lovely meal to enjoy."

Once they finished dinner, Connor went to the kitchen for more wine while Tula sat in one of the chairs beside the fireplace. He soon returned with two glasses.

"You aren't trying to get me tipsy, are you?" she teased.

"I wish that was so," Connor said with a bleak look. "There's something we should discuss."

"Oh?" Her pulse quickened in anticipation.

"There are some things you need to know about the Clares, and especially about Moira. I debated about telling you, but after what you said this afternoon, you need to know about them, and about Moira in particular."

Deflated by the serious look on his face, she puzzled over what he might say. For a moment, she hesitated, uncertain she wanted to hear what he planned to tell her. Yet she had never been one to shy away from reality, whatever it might be. She took a deep breath and waited.

"You and Moira may be more closely related than she has told you. It's likely she is your half-sister."

Stunned into shocked silence, Tula stared at Connor, unable to absorb and understand his words. Connor sat there, waiting for her response.

After a full minute passed, Tula broke the heavy silence. "Is it true? How do you know?"

Connor relaxed before answering. "One day, the year I was seven, I crept in the back door, careful to make no noise. I'd had a fight with Rory and didn't want Mam to know. I heard her talking with someone." He paused as if choosing his words with care.

"She was in the lounge with another woman. As I eavesdropped, I soon realized it was Maeve Clare, Moira's mother. She was crying, and Mam was comforting her. Maeve complained Grady had beaten her and threatened to kill Moira, who was then about my age. I never heard of a father wanting to kill his daughter before. It frightened me." Connor shook his head and looked unhappy.

Struggling to grasp all the implications of Moira's relationship to her, Tula found Connor's revelation unnerving. "You said Moira's my sister, so she wasn't this Grady's daughter."

"Yes, but I didn't know that then. As I recall, Mam told Maeve … the past was past. Moira was half-grown, and that God would strike Grady down. Then Maeve just cried harder. She told my mam that Moira had the sight. Mam sighed then, saying it hadn't helped Maeve."

"They said nothing more for a time." Connor looked down at his hands as if reluctant to continue.

"So? What happened? Moira said her father died one cold night of too much drink and froze to death on his way home from the pub. She never mentioned he had a different name from Clare."

"Indeed, that's what Maeve said of Grady, and others had seen him drinking. She said she had fixed him a hearty stew that night, but served the children something earlier. I've often wondered what was in that stew."

Aghast, Tula pondered the possible consequences. "You think she killed him?"

Connor shrugged, but said nothing for moment. After a deep sigh, he continued. "Maeve kept her maiden name, as had her mother before her. She married Grady McGinnis only for the sake of the child she then carried, but she insisted the child take the name Clare. She later did the same with Ewan. Grady hated that, but he wanted Maeve badly enough to agree. I suspect he thought he could change her mind later."

"Nothing you've said indicates that my father left Maeve with his unborn child." Tula still didn't believe her father would have left any woman, had he known about a child, his child.

"I haven't finished yet. After Maeve stopped sniffling, she spoke again. She said she and Brendan were fated, and her visions had shown them together. Then she added no one could rely on the "sight." She told Mam that the only man she'd ever loved had left, and she was carrying his child. She had to protect the wee thing not yet born.

"Mam had apparently urged Maeve to take Grady as a husband. The marriage was fine, at first, but Moira came early. Grady became suspicious and demanded Maeve tell him the name of the father. He'd even blackened Maeve's eye over it. Things didn't improve much till Ewan was on the way."

He ceased speaking.

"But the trouble didn't end there?" Tula prompted.

"Ah, no." Connor looked depressed. "When bad times came and jobs got tight, Grady took to drinking more and then to beating Maeve. She wasn't one to be meek. Later, years later, Mam told me she suspected Maeve used some of her 'cures' on Grady."

"Was that all Maeve said that day," Tula asked.

"No, she said a bit more. She said the past was the past. That whatever happened, Moira and Ewan were hers, and she'd protect her own. Maeve insisted Moira was the next generation of Clares.

"With that, Maeve left," Connor continued. "I went outside and then banged the door as I entered. I didn't want Mam to know I'd listened to her and Maeve."

Tula tried to take in all Connor had said, but it was too much. Her father was Moira's too? Moira was her … half-sister?

"Connor, why are you telling me this?"

"After what you said earlier about suspicions of Ewan and Moira, I thought you should know. I don't know what it means, but I suspect Moira knows about her real father." He ran a hand through his hair. "I had planned a different evening when I asked you to have dinner with me, but if your life is at stake, you need to know everything I can tell you."

"I … I appreciate that. Does Rory know?"

"Good God, no. I've never told anyone, and I'm certain neither Maeve nor Mam did. It's not something they would have wanted known."

"What about Moira?" Tula held her breath, waiting.

"I don't know. Maeve may have told her, or Moira might have discovered some note or something from Maeve."

At last he raised his head and looked at Tula. "We best join the others at the pub."

Tula distinctly remembered Moira saying she had known Brendan and remembered his leaving Kilconon never to return. Yet Connor said Brendan left before Moira was born. One of them lied, but which one and why. She wanted to trust them both, but her life depended on the truth, not wishful thinking.

"Connor, I don't think I can face Moira just now. Will you drop me at the cottage?"

"Are you certain you want to go there?"

"Yes, at least for tonight. I've a lot of thinking to do. Just tell Moira I'm exhausted."

* * * *

After Connor dropped her off at Moira's cottage, Tula hurried inside and made ready for bed. She didn't want to talk to either Moira or Ewan. She had to sort things out in her own mind before doing anything.

She could think of no reason for Connor to lie. Tula knew he disliked Ewan and wanted little to do with Moira. He implied that Moira had designs on him. Yet neither of those was any reason to blacken her character. Even if Moira were a half-sister, that wasn't a reason for her to kill or make her sick. Tula couldn't see what harming her would do for Moira. It made no sense.

Rory Doyle was in love with Moira and wanted to marry her. Surely, if she were vindictive or nasty, Rory would know. Thinking back, Tula recalled only one woman who had indicated she disliked Moira. At the time, Tula, too full of her discoveries of Moira's sale table of herbal remedies at the jumble sale, hadn't asked the woman why. She didn't remember the woman's name, but Father Donnelly would know it and how to contact her.

Father Donnelly hadn't been in Kilconon when Brendan left, but perhaps his housekeeper had. Surely, others would know when Brendan had left. All she had to do was find them.

Convinced someone could resolve her confusion, she drifted into restless sleep.

Chapter Twenty-One

When Tula came downstairs the next morning, she found Moira in the kitchen as usual. Struggling to appear normal, she yawned and stretched. "Morning, Moira."

"Morning, Cousin," Moira responded. "Breakfast?"

"Umm, yes. After that long van ride yesterday, I'm for a walk after breakfast."

"It's back to business for me," Moira said as she cooked the eggs. "I found a few orders online this morning."

Once Tula finished breakfast, she was determined to resolve her doubts about Connor's revelations. The problem was where to start. She had met only a few of Kilconon's residents. Even though Father Donnelly hadn't been here when her father left, he would know the names of residents who had lived here then. Still hesitating, she decided to start with Rory. By now, he would be at his shop.

She waved good-bye to Moira and closed the door behind her. In less than ten minutes, she reached Rory's shop. It was a fine day and the village sparkled after a bit of overnight rain. The air carried a hint of peat smoke, fresh blooming roses, and a touch of car exhaust. As usual, a line of wellies sat on one side of the shop door, and pitch forks and shovels leaned against the wall on the other side.

Tula opened the door to find Rory serving an older woman wearing a pink floral dress. She had a wheeled cart stacked with boxes of various foods and some canned goods. Rory added a small sack of potatoes to her cart.

"That's the lot, Mrs. O'Hara," Rory said. "Now, if you'll sign the account book, please."

The woman nodded and stepped to the counter. After signing the book, she pulled her cart toward the door, which Tula held open.

"*Gura míle*." She smiled at Tula and Rory as she left, the cart rolling along behind her.

Rory faced Tula with a welcoming smile. "Now, Miss Mohr, how can I help you?"

"It's Tula, Rory, not Miss Mohr." She grinned as she approached him. "I really appreciate the information on Irish history and your colorful stories yesterday of Cú Chulainn. They livened up the trip and helped me experience Ireland in a much fuller way. They also added to my collection of myths, legends, and folklore. I like the insights they provided to people and places."

Rory nodded. "It's a fine day when we can tell visitors about Ireland and its real history instead of the *ráiméis* shown in films. Most tourists aren't much interested in our history. They want the scenery, souvenirs, and tales of the little people." A long sigh followed.

"For me," Tula replied, "the soul of the country is what matters. I felt closer to that during our trip. Now, because of my father, I'm looking for information about Kilconon's recent history. You, Connor, and Moira were all born here."

"Connor and Moira, yes. I was born at home on the farm, but we all went to the same school. I was the oldest, then Connor, and Moira was the youngest."

"I would guess you were like three musketeers."

"Ah, no." Rory's apologetic grin surprised Tula. "Connor and I would scuffle some now and then. Boys will you know. As for Moira, she was small for her age and teased a lot by the others. There were a few called her names, and her mother as well. Maeve had a reputation of sorts then."

Moira had never discussed her childhood with Tula. "As an herb seller?"

"Well, not exactly." Rory paused a moment as if considering how to say what he meant. "Like Moira, Maeve sold herbs for illness … and … other things. She had the second sight. That scared a few."

Tula nodded, thinking of Cassie. "I have a friend who has that too. I'm curious why it bothered people. My friend's visions come as warnings."

"I know little about it. Some of the more devout church members regard it as the work of the Devil."

"Oh." Tula at once thought of the witch hunters.

"Moira always kept her head up high. After Maeve died, Connor's mam tried to help as well, but the scars are still there."

Tula guessed the teasing had probably been difficult for Moira to deal with as a child. Other children could be so cruel. She had suffered some of that herself because of her mixed heritage. Memories of other children pointing fingers at her and whispering to one another were a part of her early school days.

She took a deep breath before asking her next question. "Do you remember when my father left Kilconon?"

"I was a wee one then, but I remember Mam talked about it and visited Mrs. Mohr regularly. She was a widow by then. Your grandfather worked on a fishing boat and was lost at sea during a storm. Not much money in Kilconon, so your da went to London. He sent money home to his mam."

Her grandfather a fisherman? Her father had never mentioned that. Now she had even more questions. "How old were you?"

Rory rubbed his chin and looked thoughtful. "I might have been four or five. I'm not quite sure. Connor was an infant I think. I'm not sure if Moira had even been born yet. Maybe I'm remembering what Mam said later."

"There must still be some people in Kilconon who might remember Brendan Mohr."

Rory shook his head. "We lost most of the older ones. No Clares remain except for Moira and Ewan. Grady McGinnis, their father, died fifteen or more years ago. His sister Fiona is still here, but she's a bitter one now. Perhaps Mrs. O'Hara or Oona Dunn, Father Donnelly's housekeeper, might know. If I remember any others, I'll pass them on."

Tula nodded. So far, Rory's account appeared to confirm what Connor had told her. "Thanks for talking with me, Rory. I might see if Father Donnelly has any suggestions."

Strolling along Market Street toward the rectory, or whatever the Irish called the priest's house, Tula mulled over Rory's information about Moira. It appeared to confirm most of what Connor said, but a niggle of doubt still persisted. She passed the Kilconon Arms and several small stone houses that shared common walls. Some had broken slate roofs. The aura was anything but prosperous, although two had been freshly whitewashed. The window boxes of those held a combination of daisies and bright geraniums. At least the breeze kept the air fresh and brought the mixed scent of grasslands and peat bogs.

Approaching St. Bridgit's, Tula thought it small compared to the churches in Dingle. Opening the gate to Father Donnelly's house, she hurried toward the porch. Mrs. Dunn, the housekeeper, opened the door at Tula's knock, but didn't invite her inside. The warm smell of something baking floated from inside the house.

"Father's out just now visiting old Mrs. Johns." Mrs. Dunn looked apologetic. "She took sick after the church supper. Poor woman has no kin left. Her neighbor sent for Father Donnelly."

Another person sick at the supper? Perhaps others suffered the same stomach attack she and Geneva had endured. "A stomach ailment?" Tula suggested.

"Mercy no. She's close to ninety-three. It's her heart. She would try a jig. Always prided herself on knowing all the jigs, she did."

"How sad." Tula suppressed a smile at the image of a very old woman doing a jig.

Mrs. Dunn shook her head. "Yes and no. There comes a time for us all. It seems likely hers has arrived. Did you want to see Father?"

Tula remained silent for a moment, considering what to say and how to frame her questions. No sense in adding to gossip. "I met a woman taking cash at the jumble sale yesterday. Devlin, or some such, and she said something about my father."

Tula crossed her fingers. It was only a minor fib. After all, the woman had said she knew when her father left. "I have a few questions to ask her, but don't know where to find her."

"Yes, she helps out every year." Mrs. Dunn surveyed Tula with narrowed eyes. "Your Moira's cousin. Fiona Devlin has no love for the Clares, even if they are her kin. Still bears a grudge against all Clares over Grady's death. 'Course, I wasn't here then, so I know naught about it." Mrs. Dunn appeared to be listening to something.

Tula heard a clock chime somewhere in the house. The smell of baking bread filled the air and made Tula's mouth water.

"That'll be my bread. Is there anything else?"

Tula sighed. "It smells delicious. Can you tell me where Mrs. Devlin lives?"

"Across the bridge and the third house on."

"Thank you, Mrs. Dunn. I hope Mrs. Johns survives to dance at next year's event."

"Only the good Lord knows." The housekeeper crossed herself and closed the door.

Tula stood outside a moment before leaving the porch, pondering how to approach Fiona Devlin. After closing the garden gate behind her, she surveyed Kilconon. Beyond the shops and the last house, the picturesque stone bridge at the edge of town looked like it had been there for a hundred years or more. The grey stones looked suitably weathered yet sturdy. She remembered seeing it in one of Michael O'Brien's watercolors. On the other side of the stream were perhaps ten buildings. Some were small cottages while several were modern brick bungalows.

She walked back down Market Street. Rory was not visible this time. She soon reached the stone bridge and crossed to the narrow dirt lane on the other side.

Like so many Irish streams, the water under the bridge arch appeared brown because of its source in the peat bogs, and carried the smell of grasses and decaying vegetation. Pretty to the eyes, but less enticing to the nose. She hurried along the narrow lane to the cottages ahead. The houses here were smaller and even less well kept than those in the village proper.

The third house was a smaller edition of Moira's home with a low tin roof covered by peeling green paint. These homes sat close by the road that ran along the stream, and a stand of tall bushes rose behind them. Some window boxes held geraniums, and neat white curtains hung in a few windows. The bright blossoms must be more for their color than their scent. Tula approached the green wooden door and knocked softly.

The Devlin residence looked almost like a shotgun house. Too small for any family, but perhaps sufficient for a couple. The window boxes had the ubiquitous geraniums and a straggly rose bush grew by the door. The stoop looked newly swept.

Tula knocked at the door again and waited. The grey-haired woman from the jumble sale opened it and stared at her.

"Yes?" She eyed Tula as if wondering what she could possibly want.

"We met at the church jumble sale, Mrs. Devlin. I'm Tula Mohr."

The woman nodded. "You bought Michael O'Brien's paintings."

"Yes, and a few other things. I'm Brendan Mohr's daughter. I've come to Kilconon to see my father's birthplace. He died some years ago, but not here. It happened while I was in college, so there were many things I never was able to ask him. I came hoping to find some relatives or people who knew him. Mrs. Dunn said you've lived here all your life."

"That I have." The woman appeared puzzled. "Why don't you come in. I've just put the kettle on for tea. Would you like some?" She held the door open.

"Thank you, that sounds lovely."

Mrs. Devlin stepped back, and Tula entered a combined sitting room and small kitchen. She assumed a bedroom lay beyond. Looking around the room, it appeared spotless, but a bit crowded with a floral love seat, two dark green chairs on either side of an electric fire, and small black tables next to the chairs, it still offered comfort. Tula took the chair to the left, near the fireplace. The upholstery once had been burgundy but now appeared more brown. The electric fire wasn't on and the air, despite the warm day outside, was a bit cool.

"Good, I'll bring you a cup." Mrs. Devlin hurried to the kitchen area.

She soon returned with a tea tray she placed on one of the tables. "Milk?"

She bustled about filling two cups from a teapot covered with bright yellow cozy. She brought Tula one cup and kept the other. The lovely bone china cups surprised Tula. A pattern of roses and violets covered the sides of the fragile cups.

"What beautiful cups. They must be a family heirloom."

"Yes, my mother received them as a wedding present. I seldom have occasion to use them."

"I feel honored."

Tula sipped the hot tea and studied Fiona Devlin. The woman looked like she had experienced a hard life. Being a widow in a small village couldn't be easy. Clearly, she took pride in the heirloom cups and kept her small home tidy and welcoming.

"My father, Brendan Mohr, left Kilconon thirty or so years ago and never returned. His mother, my grandmother, died here some years back."

"Mohr? Yes, there was the Widow Mohr and a son. Can't say I know much about them."

"Oh? His mother was a Clare. Father Donnelly said Moira Clare might be my cousin."

Fiona Devlin stared at Tula with gimlet eyes. "The good Lord pity you."

Prepared for a negative reaction, Tula made a grimace. "Moira seems nice enough. She said she knew little about my father, but remembered him."

"She remembered him? Not likely. He left before she was born. Moira and Ewan are my brother Grady's children except…"

Quick to catch the implications of that pause, which seemed to confirm Connor's story, Tula waited.

Fiona sighed. "It ill becomes me to gossip about kin, but…" Another pause, this one longer. She took a deep breath. "Maeve Clare never had time for Grady, even though he bought her gifts and begged her to marry him. All of a sudden, one day, she changed her mind and they married in a hurry."

"Maeve?" Tula prompted.

"Moira's mother, she of the love potions and second sight. An evil woman who could curse or cure with ease. Most people feared her, but not Grady. He wouldn't hear a word against her. Beautiful like the dark Irish, she could have any man she wanted, but she was too proud to accept any village man. Grady loved her, so he married her."

A full minute passed before Fiona spoke again. "Moira was an eight-month baby. At first, Grady was fine, but the old women began to gossip, and then someone at the pub had too much beer. Grady beat the man for his slur against Maeve."

Tula held her silence waiting for Fiona to continue.

148

"My brother was a good man and a good father, but that night he got very drunk. When he got home, there was a terrible row. Of course, Maeve denied any wrongdoing, but after that, Grady ignored Moira. A few years later, Ewan was born and Grady was a proud father with a fine son."

Sipping the last of her tea, Tula again waited. Fiona appeared lost in memories.

"The happy times lasted a while, but one night another row occurred, and Grady beat Maeve. She wasn't one to take such lightly. The next day, Grady had stomach cramps. Then, week by week, he lost weight and grew frail. One cold night…" Fiona stopped and tears traced a silent path down her face.

The human cost of love always troubled Tula. Perhaps that was why she had always avoided close relationships. According to Connor, Maeve was driven to protect herself and her children from a violent man. Fiona saw her brother as the victim of a scheming woman. Tula reached out a hand to pat Fiona, but the old woman pulled back.

"My brother was no fool." She fixed a fierce stare on Tula. "He knew Maeve was poisoning him, but he lost the will to live. The next morning they found him by the side of the road smelling of drink and dead. Maeve killed him. The children were all called Clares, even Ewan. Grady lost his son to the *cailleach*."

Maeve, a witch? At a loss to comfort the bitter woman, Tula remained quiet. No one triumphed in tragedy. Connor said Maeve died a painful death. Moira looked to fast becoming as bitter as Fiona. Ewan had grown up fatherless, spoiled by his mother and now Moira. A tragic family.

Tula now had a sort of confirmation of Connor's story. That Moira was her half-sister could not be proven, except perhaps by DNA, but appeared likely. Tula remained uncertain what to do about it. She still didn't know why Moira had lied about knowing Brendan Mohr.

"I curse the Clares, every one," Fiona snarled.

For a moment, she stared at Tula, not really seeing her. "You're American and your father was a Mohr. In spite having a Clare for a mother, neither he nor you are Clares, leastwise not in the sense that Maeve was or that Moira and Ewan are. You should shun them before one or the other does you harm. I may not have second sight, but I know human nature. Maeve's git will have its way."

Chapter Twenty-Two

As Tula left Fiona's, she tried to sort out her feelings. None of it resolved her concerns about Moira. It appeared likely they were half-sisters, but then what? That didn't explain why Moira would want to harm her, that is, if she had tried.

In Tula's view, her cousin was a person who was not open about emotions. The only love Moira showed was for Ewan. While friendly with Rory, she showed no romantic interest in him and kept a certain distance. As for Connor, Moira had never mentioned how she felt about him, but her behavior convinced Tula she loved him, or at the least saw him as the man she wanted to marry. Connor had made it clear he wasn't interested.

Even though Kilconon was small, there had to be other men around. Moira was not yet middle-aged or homely, although she did nothing to enhance her looks. Her mother had been the village beauty, according to Fiona and Connor. If she was jealous over Connor's attention to others, how would she react? Had Moira only intended a temporary disruption and nothing more?

As Tula neared Rory's store, she saw him sitting outside his shop smoking his pipe. She waved to him and he beckoned her to join him.

"Morning, Miss Mohr." He welcomed her with a broad grin. "Out for a walk this fine day?"

"Tula, remember," she replied as she sat beside him on the wooden bench. "I went to visit Fiona Devlin."

Rory raised an eyebrow at that. "I didn't know you were friends."

"I met her at the jumble sale."

"Yes, she works there every year." He still looked puzzled.

Tula nodded. "So I understand. She's Moira's aunt."

"She's no love for Moira or Ewan either."

"Fiona said she hates the Clares. She claims Maeve killed her brother."

Rory puffed on his pipe and blew out the aromatic smoke in a slow stream. "Did she now?"

"She's a bitter woman," Tula added. "Connor told me the story of Grady."

Nodding, Rory remained silent.

"Of course, there are always two sides or even more in such situations."

"Indeed."

Rory's failure to say more bothered her. He would protect Moira no matter what. She'd have to try another approach.

"I noticed that beyond you and Connor, my cousins have few friends."

He said nothing for a moment. "Maeve always told Moira and Ewan that, as Clares, they were above others."

He paused for another puff on his pipe. The light smoke swirled and rose in a lazy spiral that faded in the air. He stared toward the church without an apparent focus.

"Maeve had a reputation. I think I told you that earlier. She claimed to have the second sight. Like Moira, she dealt in herbs, potions, and cures. Some say she also sold curses and love portions. Few believe in those any more, but the herbs worked."

That triggered thoughts in Tula of the witch trials and the dangerous power of beliefs. However, she failed to see how that affected the present.

"Kilconon is small and always has been," Rory continued. "When Moira was young, we had no pharmacies and few doctors, none here. So, many turned to Maeve. Yet the villagers regarded her with suspicion, especially if the object of a curse died. No one ever openly accused Maeve, but people only went to her when they were desperate.

"Maeve taught Moira all she knew and Maeve's reputation tainted how others regarded Moira. She's not had an easy life. You're concerned about her lack of friends. That's good of you."

Tula took a deep breath and fingered her sun pendant. "Rory, is

Moira my half-sister?" She waited for his reply, not at all certain what she wanted to hear.

He knocked out his pipe and considered the question. "I don't know. Why do you think that?"

"Connor thinks so, and Fiona insists Moira wasn't her brother's daughter."

Rory looked thoughtful. "Connor, I trust, but Fiona? Ah, she's bitter that one. She hated Maeve and now she hates Moira and Ewan." His look of disgust made his feelings clear.

"My father never spoke of Maeve or much beyond the beauty of Kilconon," Tula said. "I don't think he even knew about Moira."

A slight haze formed as Rory blew on his pipe to keep it burning. "I doubt his mam ever told him, especially after he married."

Either that or Connor was wrong. "Who would know?"

"Tula, what happens between two people is known only to them. Maeve is dead and so is your father. Does it matter now?"

His question gave her pause. Was she wrong about Moira? As an only child and then an orphan, she had longed for a brother or sister, but mostly a sister. She didn't lack friends, good friends, but that wasn't the same as family.

"I don't know."

She couldn't hint of her suspicions to Rory. He'd not believe ill of Moira. In a muddle, she began to wonder if being sisters did matter.

Tula stood and looked toward the Kilconon Arms. "I always enjoy talking to you, Rory, but I should get some lunch."

"Any time."

Hearsay wasn't always right. Sooner or later, she would have to talk with Moira. It wasn't certain that Maeve would have told her daughter who her father was. It didn't have to be Brendan.

* * * *

Tula hadn't seen Moira all day. It was now late afternoon, so she set out for a walk. Walking always helped her to sort out her problems. The mild weather made the excursion pleasant as she stopped to admire the high fuchsia hedges lining the narrow lane. Occasionally, a gated entrance to a farmer's field interrupted the barrier. The Irish didn't have sidewalks or footpaths, except in towns, villages, and tourist sites. When two cars traveling opposite directions met, one had to back to the nearest break to let the other pass. Fortunately, most vehicles traveled at an unhurried speed.

Daylight lasted a long time in the Irish summer. Tula smelled new mown hay in the air as she strolled at a leisurely pace. Ireland had plenty of green grass, but few trees. However, the tall fuchsia hedges made that lack less apparent along the road. Rory's explanation of the past deforestation by the Irish and the British remained fresh in her memory.

That brought to mind the trip to the Cliffs of Moher with Rory, Moira, and Connor. Moira had sat in sullen silence on the return trip, disappointed over the Burren restrictions, and perhaps her reaction to Rory's unwelcome proposal as well. Tula also suspected she was angry because Connor had been so attentive to her rival. He was an attractive man free of attachments, and not one Tula cared to resist. For once, she considered the prospects of sharing her life with someone—a blue-eyed Irishman like Connor Kehoe.

A horn sounded and Tula backed tight against the dense hedge. She had passed a farmer's gate a bit farther back. The black car maneuvered as far left as possible and missed her by inches. The driver waved his thanks, and she waved back.

Shortly, she reached two more farmer's gates on opposite sides of the road. Cows lowed as they passed through the one to her left, herded by an older man dressed in a rough cap and a waxed coat. Once through the barrier, the cows crossed to the other side and milled in front of the gate there.

The farmer tipped his cap as he passed. "Afternoon," he said.

He hurried ahead to unlock the other gate, and shooed the cows through, closing it behind them. Re-crossing the road, he closed the opposite one and then rejoined his herd. The herd had left evidence of their passage across the road. The pungent odor and the gooey remains made Tula careful of where she stepped.

Time was passing, and she hadn't made any progress in what to do about Moira. She could always confront her, but something held her back. If she didn't return for dinner, Moira would worry, so she decided to turn around and head back to Kilconon once she reached the next break. There, she stopped for a moment to drink from her bottle of water. She had come to prefer the water from Moira's well and hoped Mohr House had as good a well.

On the return walk, she moved to the other side of the road and had almost reached the cow crossing when the roar of a high-powered engine reached her. She pushed herself as far into the dense hedge as she could before the vehicle whooshed past. A red car. Ewan?

Suddenly, the screech of brakes was followed immediately by a loud bang. The sound of grinding metal and breaking glass shattered the evening peace. The sounds indicated at least one vehicle had been destroyed. If it was Ewan's Viper...

Chapter Twenty-Three

Tula, her heart pounding, ran toward the ominous sounds. Around a curve in the road, she stopped and stared, horrified, at the twisted wreckage of the red car. The dark haired driver was slumped over the wheel, his face buried in the deployed airbag. A mangled tractor lay on its side, the wheels still spinning. Panic struck as she approached the crunched car.

"Ewan, Ewan are you all right?" Unconscious, he didn't respond.

Uncertain how badly Ewan had been injured, Tula sought for a pulse. It beat steadily. Relieved, she released an explosive breath. He looked bruised, but she saw no obvious wounds or bleeding. Somewhat relieved, she pulled out her recently purchased, prepaid cell phone, turned it on, and fumbled as she punched the emergency number.

Within seconds, a female voice responded. "You have reached emergency services for the Dingle Peninsula. What is your emergency and position?"

"Tula Mohr, tourist…" Almost breathless, she gave the name of the lane and the approximate distance from Kilconon. With a struggle, she managed to steady her voice. "A car and tractor collided. The tractor driver looks scratched but okay. The driver of the car is unconscious and collapsed over the steering wheel of his car. Hurry, please."

"A unit is on the way. Is the driver alive?"

"I… I think so. I felt a pulse."

"Stay with the victim until help arrives."

Tula disconnected and turned to the scowling farmer. He had several scratches on his face.

He shook his head as he stared at his tractor. "Stupid tourist. No business driving them pricey, foreign toys so fast. He's gonna cop it."

"Are you all right?" Tula said.

"Me bloody tractor ain't. I want it fixed. Bloody Euros. If I hadn't jumped off, I'd be laid out dead."

Fearing Ewan might have internal injuries, Tula paced. The waiting seemed interminable. She began to pray to all the gods. No way would she call Moira until she knew how Ewan was. Fifteen long minutes passed before she heard the blaring sirens and saw the flashing lights as the emergency vehicle arrived. An Irish EMT jumped out and rushed to the car and Ewan. After a quick check, he motioned to his colleague and they debated the best way to remove Ewan from the smashed vehicle. Meanwhile, a Garda Panda car pulled up behind the EMT vehicle.

The Garda officer approached Tula. "You reported the accident, ma'am?"

"Yes, I'm Tula Mohr. I'm staying with my cousin Moira Clare in Kilconon. I was taking a stroll when I heard the accident."

"You didn't see it?"

"No. A red car raced past me and moments later, I heard the crash. I jogged to the site and found the car wrecked, and the driver, my cousin, slumped over the wheel. So, I called the emergency number. The farmer, the driver of the tractor, looked a bit shaken, but without major injuries."

"Your cousin? You weren't riding with him?"

"No, I was out for a walk. I don't think my cousin even saw me. He was driving too fast. I don't know the farmer, but the car driver is my cousin Ewan Clare."

"Umm, Mr. Clare has a number of speeding tickets. I wonder you weren't with him."

"No, once was enough. I refused to ride with him. I've never liked his driving." She grimaced at the memory.

"I see. He didn't stop when he passed you?"

"The road is narrow, and I was backed against and into hedge as far as I could go. As it was, he barely missed me."

"Umm, yes. I believe we have his address on file. I'll just ask the crew what they're going to do. I expect, because he's unconscious, they'll transport him to hospital." The police officer approached the EMTs, conferred briefly, and then returned to Tula.

"They said since you're a relative, you can ride with the victim to hospital. I have to talk with the tractor driver and examine the accident scene for my report, so you best go with them."

The burly EMTs used a crow bar and tools Tula didn't recognize to open the driver's car door. They eased Ewan from the wrecked car and then loaded him on a waiting gurney. Once they had him in their vehicle and hooked to a variety of monitors, the taller of the two EMTs approached Tula.

"We're taking the driver to hospital. He's unconscious, and needs to be checked by a doctor for any other problems. Most likely he'll be kept overnight for observation unless his injuries are more severe than they now appear. Would you care to ride along with him?"

"Thank you, I would."

He helped Tula into the vehicle and closed the door. All Tula could think of was Moira. She dreaded telling her and prayed to all the gods Ewan wasn't seriously injured.

Once at the hospital, Tula waited while doctors examined her unconscious cousin.

A long half hour later, a young man in scrubs approached her. "Miss Mohr, I'm Dr. Brennan. Your cousin, Mr. Clare, is bruised and has a concussion, but no serious injuries. We'll keep him overnight and probably release him by noon tomorrow."

"Thank you. His sister will be so relieved." Tula pulled out the cell phone and called Moira. "Ewan's had an accident." A frightened gasp sounded over the connection.

"What? An accident? Is he…"

"He's okay and at the hospital in Dingle. He may have a concussion and some cracked ribs, so they're keeping him overnight. I'll be home as soon as I can get a ride back."

"How bad?" Moira said, her voice anxious.

"Moira, I said he's all right. Nothing really serious. They're keeping him tonight only as a precaution. The doctor assured me he just had bruises in addition to the concussion. Don't worry. I'll see you shortly." Tula disconnected and went to find a taxi or bus to Kilconon. She dreaded having to deal with hysterics from Moira.

Chapter Twenty-Four

A week later, Moira stared at the white envelope addressed to Ewan. It was the kind used for business, usually in her case, to demand money. No, not now. She didn't need this.

Knitwear sales had dropped and only the money Tula contributed enabled her to buy food. At least she didn't have rent to pay. The cottage was free of any lien.

The envelope's return address was the leasing company. It could only mean one thing—they wanted Ewan to pay for the wrecked vehicle. With trembling fingers, she tore open the envelope and removed the multi-page letter with a note attached. The black words literally jumped from the page.

Complete the attached form and return with full payment.

Surely, they had insurance on leased vehicles. Why demand payment from Ewan? It wasn't even a new car. Even worse, her name was there as co-signer.

She began to laugh. The laughter soon turned to wracking sobs. If only she hadn't agreed to letting him lease such an expensive car. Why hadn't she just said no?

Moira thanked his luck that Ewan had survived the crash, but cursed at what it now left. She didn't have that amount of money, nor did anyone she knew. The only things of value she had were her store and the cottage. Her only hope lay with borrowing the money from Tula, but would even she have that amount of money?

* * * *

Overjoyed at Rory's news about the possible purchase of Mohr House, Tula returned from seeing him, ready for a celebratory lunch. She must to make a list of all the repairs needed. If the owner accepted her offer, Rory said the work on the roof could begin almost at once.

She found Moira in the kitchen staring at papers on the table as if they were something to fear. Her skin was ashen and her eyes red as if she had been crying.

"Are you all right? Has something happened to Ewan?"

"No." The lost soul look on Moira's face worried her.

"You're not all right or Ewan's not?"

Moira sighed. "We're both fine." She filled the teakettle and began the preparations for making tea. "We have some of the leftover stew I'm going to heat it for lunch if that's okay."

"Suits me."

Something had upset Moira and it could only be Ewan or money. Ewan appeared to have survived the crash with no major injuries, so that left money. Had the bank or creditors demanded payment? So far as Tula knew, Moira owed money to too many people. Then she realized it had to be about the wrecked car.

Moira placed the full teapot in front of Tula. "The stew won't take a minute."

Tula poured the tea and decided to wait until after lunch to pursue the source of Moira's distress. The savory smell of the stew filled the kitchen and made her mouth water. Moira was a great cook.

Soon, Moira set a plate before Tula. The stew was even better than the first time. After they finished the stew and a plate of current scones, Moira added a fresh pot of tea.

"Now, tell me the problem," Tula said.

"It's ... it's the leasing company. They want Ewan to pay for the car." Moira stared down into her tea.

"Let him pay," Tula said. "It's his debt."

"It's mine too. I co-signed." She looked up at Tula, tears sliding down her face. "They'll take the cottage and the shop."

"Moira, you need a lawyer, barrister, or whatever they call them here. I'm sure the leasing company is interested in getting their money, not in taking your home. As for Ewan, he needs some tough love. It's past time you insisted he pay his debts. He created this mess, so let him get a job and pay the leasing company. Neither you nor I wrecked the car, and neither of us should foot the bill."

Sighing, Moira shook her head. "Yes, all that may be true, but I'm liable too."

"I don't understand this at all." Tula studied her cousin's troubled face. "Even in the States, the Viper is an expensive car. I never met anyone who owned one."

"You know how charming Ewan can be. He convinced the leasing people that having a handsome young man driving one in the tourist season, when all the Europeans, Americans, and others are here, would be good advertising. In a sense, he was working for the leaser. They charged him a nominal lease rate."

"And now they want payment for the car."

"It wasn't even a new car," Moira continued. "It had been in an accident and they repaired it, but now they're demanding the full purchase price of a new one."

"It sounds like a good lawyer might be able to make a case."

"Lawyers want money upfront. I don't have any."

"What about contingency fees? Some lawyers will take a case for a share of any damages awarded."

"Damages?"

"Pain and suffering, loss of your good name. You countersue."

Moira looked thoughtful. "I don't think it works that way here."

"Whatever happens, you need legal advice and fast."

Chapter Twenty-Five

Ewan looked at the crumpled wreck of his beautiful car. The leasing company had sent Moira a whopping bill. She didn't have the money and he certainly didn't. He shouldn't have bullied her into that lease. He had wanted the car so badly that he was willing to do or say anything. He knew the leasing company was a front for the Spanish gangs, but he could have everything he wanted in return for a few favors.

There was only one way to get them to lay off, but it involved a risky trip. If he could make it to the island and back, the owners of the cargo would pay handsomely for the service. They made it all too clear that if he didn't deliver, they would demand full payment for the bloody car.

Why had he ever listened to the oily bloke when he first met him? The deal had sounded perfect. Just pick up a few small packages from the wee islands and deliver them to an agent in Tralee. Of course, he'd need a fast boat and a fast car.

When he saw the Viper, he said yes. It was the perfect car for a Clare. It impressed all the women and was the envy of every man. How could anyone refuse? He felt like a king driving it. Sure now, there was the lease with a monthly payment to convince others it was an honest deal. The payment was a bit much, but manageable, or had been until things went bad. Moira had agreed to co-sign. The bloke claimed that was merely to ensure he kept the bargain. Now, the Garda had made the pickups dangerous and seized several ships carrying drugs. As a consequence, they had resorted to smaller fishing vessels. He had put himself and Moira at risk.

He knew better than to ask Connor. That goody-goody wouldn't lift a finger to help and neither would that bitch Tula Mohr. She wouldn't part with one of her American dollars to help a Clare. He clenched his fists. Killing her would be so satisfying, but then there would be trouble getting her money. Moira seemed to think that as her nearest relations, the courts would give it to them. Anything to do with law took forever and a day. Too bad. No, he needed money and he needed it now.

A wee boat trip would do it, but it had to be soon. If he didn't retrieve the goods, some stupid tourist might stumble on them, and then where would they be?

Ewan ground out his cigarette. He better get a ride from Rory or Mal to Dingle.

* * * *

Moira stared at the steam rising from the tea in front of her. As she watched, a vision formed, slowly at first as the mist thinned. A dark sea glistened beneath a gibbous moon. A tiny boat raced over choppy waves, leaving a spreading wake behind. A rocky shore with jagged tentacles of rock reaching out to the sea lay ahead. Then the arrow-straight path of the craft changed to a zigzag pattern. The wee vessel swung, first right, and then left as it darted along the coast, seeking an opening in the rocky barrier.

A blood red light drew her attention away from the skiff. A dark behemoth bore down on its prey. The ghoulish light came from reflected moonlight in its eye. The leviathan was fast catching up to the fleeing craft.

Suddenly, a *bean sidhe* howl split the air. Moira covered her ears. Horror filled her. The last time she heard that awful cry was the night her mother died. It always signaled the end of a Clare. For whom did it howl? Her? Ewan? Tula?

The vision faded with one last mournful shriek.

Moira sat back, bewildered and fearful. The steam had abated. She shuddered and sipped the lukewarm tea. The frail vessel hunted by the monster signified something or someone, but what or who? Who was in the boat? Her dread intensified.

Worry caused the vision she told herself. The *bean sidhe*, herald of the Morrigan, remained in vivid memory. Once heard, never forgotten, but for whom did it mourn?

Its call must be for her.

Moira slumped in her chair as large tears trailed down her face.

* * * *

So far, things had gone Ewan's way. He had slipped out of the harbor in his boat as clouds aided him to avoid any Garda patrols. The familiar salt tang of the sea brought by the onshore breeze energized him. An easy trip, this. The motor purred along and water sped past the hull. No big waves tonight, just gentle swells.

Once he reached the island—more rock than land—locating the goods had presented no problem. Now underway again, he had only to avoid the Garda patrols and slip into a sheltered cove. Then he could arrange for pickup and collect his payment. All risks considered, he would demand double the usual sum.

Unfortunately, while he located the cargo, the cloud cover had abated and the waning moon had a strange red light. He suspected Moira would say it foretold misfortune for some poor sailor tonight. It was on a night such as this that Sean Mohr had died. As a Clare, such would never happen to him.

He eased away from the shore, keeping the throttle three-quarters closed to creep along to the edge of the island. So far, he'd seen no sight of the Garda patrol boats or the spotter aircraft they sometimes used. He rounded the last bit of land and opened the throttle. The boat flew like a bird, skipping over the tops of the waves. Behind, the quarter moon bathed the wake in a sickly red.

More than halfway to the cove, the bright beam from a search light suddenly hit the boat. "Jesus be damned," Ewan groaned.

He gunned the engine and gained a bit. With luck and daring, he could pull it off. Once at the cove, he would fade into the landscape and make his delivery.

He pushed the throttle as far as it could go and ducked down. The search light stayed with him as the patrol boat roared closer behind him. Ewan began to veer right and then left to make it difficult for the larger boat to track his course.

The dark rocks of the coast hove into view. So close. Not far now. He threw the gear and lifejackets overboard to lighten the load and plunged ahead. The treacherous rock outcroppings reached hungrily for the boat. At the last moment, he spun the wheel and avoided them.

One more inlet to go.

The roar of the patrol boat increased. In quick glimpses, Ewan could see the crew as white blobs lining the rails.

"STOP!" an amplified voice roared over the water. "Stand down for inspection. Now!"

Ewan ignored the order and slipped around the last line of rocks. Almost there. He urged the boat forward and didn't kill the throttle. He needed every ounce of speed. He glanced back. The patrol boat was closing on his wake.

"Stop, or you'll crash!" an officer shouted.

Ewan ignored him and aimed straight ahead at full throttle. The land rushed toward him. At the last second, he swung the wheel.

The boat didn't answer the helm.

He stared in disbelief as the boat raced toward the rocky wall ahead.

Chapter Twenty-Six

Connor called from Dingle for Moira. She stood transfixed, the phone in her hand. The stricken look on her face scared Tula.

"Moira, what is it?"

"It's Ewan," she gasped. "He's ... he's dead." Ashen faced, she dropped the phone and burst into tears.

Before Tula could respond, a loud knock sounded at the door. She hurried to answer it.

White faced, Rory stood outside. "Connor called me. Where's Moira?" he demanded.

"Shocked. I'm not sure she's grasped it yet. Come in. She's in the kitchen."

Rory pushed past Tula and she followed him into the kitchen.

He enfolded Moira in his arms. "There, there," he crooned and held her close.

She sobbed on his shoulder. Her hopeless weeping touched Tula deeply. Despite her dislike of Ewan, his death troubled her. So young to die. Moira had built her entire life around him. How would she cope now?

Unprepared for such news, she was thankful for Rory's presence. She had no idea how to comfort Moira. At a loss, she put the kettle on for tea. When the kettle boiled, Tula made the tea and set the pot and all the fixings on the table. She poured a cup for Moira and signaled Rory. He led Moira to the table and pulled out her chair. She remained standing, not responding. Gently, he urged her to sit and added milk and plenty of sugar to the tea.

"Here, Moira, drink this." Automatically, Moira accepted the cup with shaking hands and raised it slowly to her lips.

"She's in shock," Tula whispered. Rory nodded.

"A bit of whiskey might help," he half whispered to Tula.

She nodded and grabbed a bottle from the cupboard. She added some to Moira's cup and then poured him a cup and fixed one for herself. He pulled his chair close to Moira and held her hand.

"I heard the *bean sidhe*," Moira said in a toneless voice. "It always howls when a Clare dies. Ewan was a Clare. He's dead. The *bean sidhe* marked his passing."

A banshee? Poor Moira. Her woodenness and ashen face worried Tula.

"Ah, Moira, he's with Maeve," Rory said as he squeezed her hand. "Don't grieve. No one can hurt him now. Maeve protects her own." He paused a moment. "I'm here. Moira, I won't leave you."

A loud knock sounded at the door. Tula rose and went to answer it. Connor stood there, his face solemn. He slipped in and shut the door behind him. She stared at him, relieved he had come.

"How's Moira?"

"She's in shock. Rory's with her. What happened?"

"As far as I can gather, Ewan was trying to recover drugs, but the Garda were waiting for him. They gave chase and Ewan tried to escape. He ran into the rocks at full speed and died instantly."

"He died for money? For a stupid car?" Tula gaped at him. She'd had no idea Ewan was into the drug trade.

"Yes, for money. I guess, for once in his life, he intended to pay his debts. Moira could never have paid for the wrecked car, not even with Rory's help." Connor shook his head. "The drug route never works. He tried to get me involved, but I refused. I'd lose my boat, my master's license, and my business. Ewan never had any sense. He thought the Clares were above the law."

Tula rubbed her arms, suddenly cold. "Would you like some tea? I made a pot. It's in the kitchen." She led the way.

When Moira saw Connor, she jumped to her feet. "What happened?"

Connor repeated what he'd said to Tula.

"No, no. Ewan wouldn't do that," Moira insisted. "Not Ewan. He didn't touch drugs."

"Desperate men do desperate things," Tula said.

Moira stared at her with icy eyes. "You! You're the cause of all this with your stingy ways. You're no kin. You wouldn't help us. If you had, Ewan wouldn't be dead."

Shocked, Tula shook her head. "We may be related, Moira, but that doesn't mean I have to pay for Ewan's stupidity."

Moira flushed and then paled. "I curse you, Tula Mohr. May you rot in hell." She spat at her.

Tula shrugged off the curse. Moira was too emotional to hear reason. Best to say and do nothing.

Instead, Tula's silence appeared to enrage Moira further. "I hate you. You've taken everything from me. You have my father's name, his love, all he could give. You refused to share his wealth with us. You wouldn't help us. Then you took Connor. He's not yours. I thought if you should die... Well, the courts would see us as the heirs, but you wouldn't die. Nothing I tried worked."

Aghast, Tula stared at Moira, unable to absorb what she heard. So, her cousin had really tried to kill her.

"You killed Ewan," Moira snarled.

Whirling around, she grabbed a butcher knife from the counter. Tula had seen her use the knife to cut a chicken apart. Sharp, it glittered in Moira's hand.

She swung toward Tula. Raising the knife high, a maniacal look on her face, she rushed at Tula.

Rory grabbed for Moira's wrist and squeezed.

For an instant, everything froze.

Then, the knife fell from her fingers and quivered, embedded in the floor. Moira burst into broken-hearted sobs.

Rory cradled her to his chest and stroked her hair. "There, there, *a stór*. Come with me."

Stunned, Tula watched as Rory, his arm about Moira, half-led, half-carried her to the sitting room and eased her down onto the sofa. He crooned softly in his melodious voice.

It sounded like "*coo coo ru*." The tune was an Irish lullaby she remembered her father singing to her. Rory continued to stoke Moira's hair and sing in a low voice as her choking sobs began to subside.

Chapter Twenty-Seven

Connor pulled Tula away. "We'd best leave her to Rory. Right now, I'm worried about you. Let's go to the pub and get you something to eat and drink. I'm sure you could use something stronger than tea."

Shocked back to herself, she nodded, suddenly chilled to the bone. Shaken to her core, she shivered as her mind replayed the attack. Moira's grief was no surprise, but to blame her for Ewan's death made no sense. She could only hope her cousin would realize she had nothing to do with Ewan's actions.

Connor ushered her out of the cottage and into his van. Once settled, he drove the short distance to the Kilconon Arms. When they reached the pub, he led her inside and seated her close by the fire. Only a few customers remained and they were all clustered at the bar talking to one another and Jenny.

Taking her hand, his look of concern increased. "Your hands are like ice. I'll get you a drink." He chafed her cold hands with his warm ones.

Tula managed a weak smile at his efforts. "A single malt would be fine."

After he left, Tula held her hands toward the welcome warmth of the glowing fire. Moira had stunned her with her ferocious attack. She hadn't caused Ewan's death. She hadn't even been on his boat. Ever.

She stared into the glowing peat fire, reliving that awful moment. How could Moira blame her? Here, she was safe. Slowly, the warmth soothed her troubled spirits.

Connor returned with two single malts and handed one to Tula. "You need this."

She nodded and sipped the smoky liquid gratefully. "No one ever tried to kill me before."

He frowned and then sipped his drink. "Don't think about it. Moira took out her anger and frustration on you. There's no way she can blame you."

As the warmth of the single malt and the fire began to thaw the ice in her blood. She stared at him, seeking an answer. "Why?"

He frowned and sipped his drink before responding. "Loss, grief, envy, jealousy. All of them. Ewan was the center of her life."

"I didn't send him on that trip."

"No one did. He was desperate. In his favor, he didn't want Moira to deal with his debt. He'd been warned the Garda were on patrol, but he thought he could outrun them. So much for Irish charm and bravado. Cú Chulainn, he wasn't."

"I wouldn't give her the money for that damned car Ewan wrecked." Tula tried to replay the scene.

"It wouldn't have mattered if you had. Sooner or later, what happened tonight would have happened anyway. Ewan wanted the easy life, but refused to work for it. He was lucky to have avoided the Garda for so long, to say nothing of the scurvy crowd he dealt with. Moira spoiled him. She has to share the blame for his death. It's easier to blame you than to acknowledge that."

Tula nodded and sipped her drink. The chill in her veins subsided a bit more.

"You need something to eat. Jenny says they have Irish stew left. It's one of their best dishes. Maybe you'll join me in having it."

Suddenly hungry, Tula nodded.

Connor signaled Jenny and she hurried over with two plates of the stew.

Fragrant steam rose to make Tula's mouth water. The stew was tasty and filling. She ate every morsel before she sat back, replete.

"You're right. That was the epitome of Irish stew. I feel better." She took a deep breath to steady herself. "Moira accused me of stealing her father's love. I guess that means she believes she's my half-sister?" Connor nodded.

"I always wanted a brother or sister." She smiled ruefully and sipped her drink. "I didn't steal you." She looked into his eyes, now the color of stormy seas.

170

"No. I never gave Moira any reason to believe I cared for her other than as a friend. I knew Rory loved her. He's my mate. Moira never appealed to me."

"I did refuse to give her or Ewan money."

"Ewan was a lost cause, Tula. Believe me, Rory tried to talk with him and so did others. He never listened. Rory has been helping Moira out for years, but even he has his limits."

"Well, I guess I had better find another place to live."

Connor smiled and patted her hand. "Now, you have to make a decision. Where do you plan to sleep tonight? You can't go back to Moira's."

Tula stared at him. Of course he was right. The question was where.

"As I see it," Connor continued, "you could take a room here or go back to Dingle. It really depends on how you see your future."

"My future?" Tula frowned at him, confused.

"Whether you plan to stay and make Ireland your home, or go back to the States. Are you still interested in Mohr House?"

"Uh, I am, but I really hadn't thought about whether to apply for residency yet."

She bit her lip and considered what kind of a future she wanted. Would Moira change her mind and stop blaming her for Ewan's folly? Only time, and perhaps Rory, could tell. Meanwhile, what about Connor? He fascinated her, and she knew she could love him so easily, yet he hadn't indicated he felt that way about her.

"There is another option," Connor said. She focused on him, wondering what he meant.

"I have a spare bedroom and you could stay with me, at least for a while. That way you could pursue your plans for Mohr House and I could help you."

Tula tried to read his face, however his eyes gave nothing away. "Exactly what did you have in mind?"

"First, I don't think you should be alone tonight. Second, we never got to look at those maps." He wore a sheepish grin. "I promise not to force my attentions on you. You'd be free to come and go as needed. We're sensible adults and know our own minds."

Sorely tempted, Tula hesitated. Now she could understand Leah's fear and concern over Arboc, and Cassie's of Harrison. The old Tula would have said yes. Where had her self-confidence gone? Yet tonight she needed a warm pair of sympathetic arms to hold her and reassure her the future would hold no more such attacks.

"You're right. I do need someone, if only to hold me and tell me it will be okay."

"Then you'll come?" Tula nodded.

"I'll detour by Moira's and pick up your belongings. You can never tell what she might take into her head to do, although I'm sure Rory would stop her."

"Yes, that's probably the best thing to do."

They reached Moira's five minutes later and Connor went inside. He returned shortly with Tula's case and they drove to Connor's house. Once inside, he turned on the electric fire and settled her on the sofa.

Thoughts of the evening after the Cliffs of Moher when he had fixed dinner returned. It had ended so differently from what she had expected. Moira had spoiled it, but tonight she had brought them together.

They sat side by side. Connor reached over and took her hand. "You're still chilled."

She answered him with a grimace. "It isn't everyday someone tries to kill me."

"You're safe now." He put his arm around her and pulled her closer. "Does this help?"

His warmth, the smell of the sea, and the masculine scent of him comforted her. He was a man who would cherish and protect the woman he loved. For once, a man understood her need.

She nuzzled his neck as he caressed her hair and hummed softly. Gradually warmth and reassurance flowed from him to her. Nothing could hurt or threaten her. If only this would never end.

"You're a desirable woman. I sensed that from the moment I saw you at the airport. Then, after Jerome bumped you and I caught you, I decided I had to know more about you."

His words warmed her and she smiled at the memory. "I'm so sorry to have turned into this quivering mess. I'm not like this." She hardened her voice. "I won't let fear of anything or anyone rule my life."

"Fear when threatened is a natural reaction. It will pass. By tomorrow you'll laugh at it."

"I hope so." She mulled over his words and the events. Her future lay ahead, not behind.

For a while, she tried to relax and not think at all. The fear abated, but would not release her. She had to blot out all memory of hate and death. It was time to embrace life to the full.

"Connor, what I'm about to ask you may shock you and, if the answer is no, then you'd best take me to the Kilconon Arms. I'm sure I can get a room there."

"You don't want to be alone. There's no reason to leave." His look of mixed concern and disappointment didn't surprise her.

She braced herself before continuing. "Connor ... Connor, will you make love to me?"

Surprised, he held her face in his hands and studied it intently. Then, he pulled her into a tight embrace and kissed her. His tongue traced her lips and then parted them to slip inside and seek hers. He finally had to break the kiss so they could both breathe. His hands roamed over her back in slow motion, then with increased urgency. His breath caressed her ear with unmistakable desire.

Tula moved his hand to her breast, determined to make this night one they would both treasure.

"Upstairs, woman. There's a comfortable bed waiting for us."

Chapter Twenty-Eight

Two months later, Tula walked through Kilconon toward the beach, determined to get some exercise. As she neared Rory's shop, he called to her. He was sitting on a bench outside and smoking his pipe. The fragrant smoke wafted away on the slight breeze.

"Good day, Miss Mohr." His face crinkled in a welcoming smile. "Could I have a word with you?"

"How's Moira," Tula asked as she sat next to Rory. She had not seen her cousin since Ewan's funeral.

"I've a request from her," Rory said. He took a puff on his pipe and released the smoke in a gray spiral. "She saw the announcement about you and Connor applying for a license to marry."

"Oh." Tula remained quiet for a moment, imaging how Moira might have reacted. "Is she angry?"

Rory, his gaze focused on the church, said nothing for a long moment. After several more puffs on his pipe, he sighed.

"She's a deep one. It's taken some doing to convince her she wasn't responsible for Ewan's death. By the way, that leasing company has released her from all obligations."

"That's good to hear. It sounded somewhat shady to me."

"Indeed. Some Spanish group or other owned it. They ceased business."

Glad for Moira, Tula still wanted to know how things stood with her cousin. She could only hope her cousin wouldn't be like Fiona. It would be uncomfortable living in Kilconon if Moira remained a bitter enemy. Connor's home was here and she couldn't move Mohr House.

"She wants to see you."

"What?" Tula stared at Rory, unable to guess what Moira might want, but certain she didn't want to be near the woman who had tried to kill her.

"You know my feelings for her." Rory searched her face before saying more.

Tula nodded. Rory had loved Moira since childhood and supported her in so many ways. It was fortunate he had been there when Moira had attacked. Tula shuddered at the unsettling memory.

"We've applied for a license to wed."

His news stunned Tula. She would never have thought Moira would relent and marry Rory. She only hoped it was not just because of the money Moira owed him. Rory deserved better.

"Congratulations. I'm happy for both of you."

"Would you stop by her cottage tomorrow? She wants to apologize. It's important to her. You're the only family she has left."

Did Moira still consider her family? Had the attack just been Moira's reaction to Ewan's death? Her tirade had implied so much more.

Yet, family. The word resonated for Tula with deep echoes. She had lost hers. She had good friends, but they weren't family. Finding Moira and Ewan had filled her with joy at first. As for Ewan, he was charming when it suited him, but too often obnoxious and careless of others. He wasn't what she wanted in any relative. In the end, Moira had claimed Brendan as her father, so they were half-sisters. After all that had transpired, could they really be family?

As if sensing her ambivalence, Rory spoke. "She's a changed woman, Tula. She no longer hates you. I'll stay close by. Please say yes."

* * * *

In Moira's cottage the next morning, Tula watched her half-sister stare into the red glow of the electric fire as the two sat in the lounge having morning tea. The invitation via Rory had surprised Tula, especially when he almost begged her to see Moira. They had not spoken since Moira attacked her.

"Tula, thank you for coming. I … I want to … to tell you how sorry I am for … blaming you for Ewan's death. Mam insisted Ewan was the Clares' future. Her sole goal was to protect and nurture him. If he died,

175

so did the Clares. Before she passed, she made me promise to honor the Clare name and to raise Ewan as she would."

"That wasn't fair to you," Tula protested.

Connor and Rory had both told Tula what a hard, unbending woman Maeve Clare had been. For Maeve to treat her daughter so shocked Tula. Teenage Moira had done her best to raise Ewan, but Maeve was so wrong.

Moira shrugged. "There was no one else except Aunt Fiona and she hated me. I tried to do as Mam asked, but I failed her and Ewan. Rory has helped me to see I'm as much to blame as anyone for what happened. If only Mam and I hadn't given into Ewan so much, maybe he'd still be here."

Tears trembled at the corners of her eyes. She hastily picked up the teapot and poured each of them a second cup of tea. She focused on serving Tula. Only then, did she sit back and sip her tea.

"I made the scones this morning," she added.

"Umm, they smell wonderful."

For one wild moment, Tula wondered if they might be poisoned. No. Rory was sure Moira no longer hated her. She touched the golden sun pendant she wore, refusing to be held hostage by silly fears. All that lay in the past. She lived in the present.

After taking a deep breath, Tula broke open a warm scone, added fresh butter with a little wild berry jam, and took a bite. No bitter tang. She sighed, glad to let go of suspicions.

"My compliments," Tula said to Moira. "These are wonderful."

"It's Mam's recipe. She always made the best."

They sat in silence for a few moments longer, then Moira spoke again. "I'm sorry I lied to you about your father."

Tula inhaled sharply and leaned forward. "What do you mean?"

"He left Kilconon before I was born. You were a rich American, and Ewan and I... We were just scraping by. I wanted you to stay, and I thought maybe as a cousin you might help us." Moira studied the milky surface of her tea. "I'm not sure what I expected. At one point, I hoped you might marry Ewan." She sighed and then looked up at Tula. "You both had other ideas."

Ewan's death was so useless, but then so was his short life. Moira had struggled to do her best. She was just too soft. Ewan had needed a strong hand and discipline, not coddling.

Realizing this meeting must be difficult for Moira, Tula sought for comfort to offer, but the woman had lied and then tried to kill her. She could still see the sharp carving knife in her dreams. She touched her pendant again and her confidence returned.

"What's done is done." Moira looked resigned. "The truth is we're half-sisters." Tears threatened, but after a deep breath, she continued. "I lied because ... because it would have shamed Mam and pleased Fiona to tell the truth of it. She always hated Mam and me."

Setting her cup down, Moira faced Tula with a grim face. "Grady wasn't such a prize. He beat Mam and me. He was angry with her. Only Ewan's arrival pleased him, but then he accused Mam of being too easy on Ewan." She stared down into her almost empty cup. An uneasy silence reigned.

For once, Tula had no answers ready. After her own parents' death, she had built an impenetrable shell around herself. Mario had come close to piercing that. Only Connor had really touched her, and that came only after her life was threatened.

She pitied Moira. Her life had not been easy. Loss hurt so much. Perhaps the loss of Ewan cut more deeply for her half-sister than any trifling loss Tula had suffered since her parents had died. Then, she had vowed no one would ever hurt her again. Only Mario had come close.

With Cassie and Leah, she had formed firm friendships and now? Now, she was starting over again, but this time with Connor.

Staying in Kilconon meant putting down roots. Could it also mean a family? She had always wanted a sister. Could she be one to Moira? Despite Ewan, Moira had always been alone. Maeve had done her daughter no favor beyond giving her life.

"Rory has asked me to marry him," Moira said. "He's waited a long time. With Ewan gone, there are no Clares. I said yes." Her eyes brimmed with tears. "He's stood by me through everything. He was there when I needed money and when I needed someone who never judged me. At first, I didn't appreciate him because I was so focused on Connor and ... Ewan."

"Rory loves you. He told me he has loved you since you were

children."

"Yes, I just sort of took him for granted. It's taken me a long time and Ewan's death for me to realize I really do love him. You can't buy love like his."

"I'm happy for both of you." Tula reached over and took Moira's hand. "Perhaps you and Rory can have a child. With Rory for a father and you as a mother, a child would honor both the Doyles and the Clares. Maeve would be pleased to have a granddaughter."

Moira blinked as she absorbed the idea. "A granddaughter? I ... I never thought of that."

"I'd be an aunt," Tula added.

"Indeed, and I would have a child to love." Moira focused on pouring more tea.

"Sister, I have a favor to ask," Tula began. "Would you be a witness for me at my wedding?"

"You and Connor?"

"Yes. You and I are the only ones left of the Clares or Mohrs."

"Oh, Sister, yes!" Moira embraced Tula.

Salty tears flowed from each and mingled into one flow as the two women cried.

* * * *

After registering their intent to marry three months before, Tula and Connor now stood before the Dingle Registrar flanked by Moira and Rory as witnesses. Tula wore a blue silk caftan with gold embroidery around the neck, sleeve edges, and the hem that matched the blue of Connor's eyes and his tie. His gray suit fit the occasion. He had left off his familiar captain's cap revealing his dark hair.

Moira, her black hair swept up into a twist, looked lovely in a lace-trimmed white dress capped by a gossamer Shetland lace shawl, while Rory was the epitome of an Irish farmer in his white shirt and best black suit. He gave Tula a tremulous smile and tugged at his shirt collar.

Definitely a momentous day for them all. A day both Tula and Moira had never thought to see.

Cassie McLeod and Leah Muccino stood behind the couples. They had come to see Tula marry. That her best friends would make the trip pleased her. Donny, Connor's boat boy, had also come, cap in hand. Jenny would have come, but she had stayed in Kilconon to ready the reception feast at the Kilconon arms.

The Registry office was just that, a place of business dedicated to maintaining all the records of the Dingle peninsula population. While they could have chosen other venues, even a church, neither Tula nor Connor felt that necessary. Moira would never agree to a church wedding. For both couples, the signing of the required documents was unnecessary, but sufficient. The celebration later at the Kilconon Arms would allow them to share their happiness with others from the village.

Tula paused a moment to look into Connor's sea blue eyes. Once committed, there would be no turning back. She loved him unstintingly and had no regrets. He loved her and had shown that again and again.

She took the pen, signed quickly, and passed it to Connor. Their hands touched briefly, sending that delightful tingling throughout her body. Connor finished signing.

Moira and Rory then signed the required documents as witnesses.

The couples changed places and Rory and Moira signed their marriage forms, which Tula and Connor signed as witnesses.

A deep kiss from Connor left Tula breathless. When he broke the kiss, his words brushed her ear. *"Amach ó chroi, á stor."*

"Mo ghrá," Tula responded, much to Connor's surprise.

Only a kiss on the cheek from Rory, and a hug from Moira kept her from clinging to Connor. Tula turned to her friends. Cassie and Leah rushed forward to embrace her in a three-way hug.

"I never thought this day would come," Leah said, shaking her head.

"I didn't either," Cassie echoed as she wiped away tears. "I'm so happy for you both."

"Thank you for coming," Tula said. "It means a lot to mean me." Both wore the ring shawls she had sent them.

"No way would we miss it," Leah replied. "You're married, have a sister, and are starting a new business. You can sign Ted and me up as customers when you open Mohr House."

"Wonderful. I hope Cassie and Ian will come too. Having good friends, and now family, makes my life complete." Cassie and Leah both laughed.

After catching her breath, Leah spoke. "According to the cards, there's more to come."

"Such as?" Tula stared at Leah wondering what she meant.

"You'll see soon enough. Now, it's time we adjourn to that reception and celebrate."

About the Author

Nell DuVall aka Mel Jacob lives in southern Ohio with two cats, plenty of wild birds, rabbits, and squirrels. A world traveler, she has written a variety of books including time travel romance, romantic suspense, speculative fiction, nonfiction, and children's books. She reviews for two websites covering speculative fiction, including fantasy, urban fantasy, and science fiction. She is also active in the Internet Writing Workshop and on Facebook.com.

Mel Jacob (Melduvall@aol.com)--Mystery, romance, and beyond
www.Nellduvall.com

Other Works by the Author with Melange

Beyond the Rim of Light
Corpulent Chiropteran in Curious Hearts Anthology
Saving Marta in Christmas Wishes 2012 Anthology
Saving Christmas in Warm Christmas Wishes Anthology
The Three Gifts of Christmas, Holiday Hopes Anthology
Selvage
Murder in her Dreams, Book 1 of the Murder in the Shadows Series
Murder in the Cards, Book 2 of the Murder in the Shadows Series